MW00452006

AWAKENING

BY PEGGY SEALFON

To Patrick, my love…

who gives me the remarkable opportunity
to express myself and keeps me laughing through life.

To be what? To be alive, to be peaceful, to be joyful, to be loving.
And that is what the world needs most.

–Thich Nhat Hanh

ISBN-978-0-9963666-4-9 (paperback)

ISBN-978-0-9963666-5-6 (eBook)

Library of Congress Control Number: 2020948893

Cover design and book layout by Marilu Garbi

Edited by Beth Preddy

Published by Stonewater Studio Books, 2020

CONTENTS

CHAPTER ONE

*B*rakes squealed loudly, tires skidded on the asphalt leaving black
streaks of rubber… and then a deafening crash, the horrific sounds
of vehicles colliding. In a flash of time and space, Robin Stevens lay
motionless on the roadway next to her motorcycle in a cruel, life-
altering twist of fate.

The Southwest Florida air at 7 a.m. had been crisp and clear when
Robin had started up her baby blue Harley Davidson Sportster.
The sunrise painted the sky in brushstrokes of warm orange hues,
offsetting the sultry blue backdrop of the nighttime sky transitioning
into day. It was another sun-kissed Sunday in Naples and Robin had
arranged as usual to meet Richard for an adventurous ride through
the Everglades, one of the world's natural wonders overflowing with
swamps, wildlife, and dirt roads that were thrilling to explore. With
her typical enthusiasm, Robin had been giddy with excitement to see
Richard.

Richard Pendall was fun to be with and was GQ-handsome, dreamy
and tall, dark, and foreign. He had been born on the outskirts of
Paris 39 years ago and was now a much sought-after model for films
and print. Robin felt a strong connection with him bordering on a
relationship. She melted into a silly teenager when he bestowed her
with his beaming smile that crinkled the corners of his warm blue
eyes. There was a certain *je ne sais quoi* in dating a younger, super
good-looking man.

At 45, Robin was exceptionally youthful. Most people thought she was at least a decade younger than her years. A risk-taker by nature, Robin considered herself invincible and motorcycling was a lifetime passion. She believed there was little comparable to the freedom of riding in the open air, being immersed in the elements of the day, passing through sweeping landscapes with touches of wind, and even the hint of sulfur filling her nostrils before a rainstorm. With the vibrations and sounds of the engine purring beneath her athletic body, she owned the world, especially being able to control the powerful beast. Conservative friends criticized her escapades for being dangerous and unbefitting a middle-aged woman. She didn't care what they gossiped about her. Her spirit was childlike, and she wanted to soar. She loved the exhilaration of a carefree motorcycle ride. That is, until that day.

Her concession to caution was that no matter how high the temperatures climbed—and it could get brutally hot in the tropical climate—she wore leathers: a fitted jacket, black leather pants, gloves, and boots. And she was adamant about using a helmet. She often claimed, "Any biker who doesn't wear a helmet has nothing to protect."

Her straight, chestnut hair was fashioned into a single braid that flowed down her back from underneath her top-of-the-line silver helmet. She had creamy skin with a slight tan that contrasted with her pale brown almond shaped eyes looking out from behind protective goggles. She wasn't beautiful but extremely attractive with a fun-loving nature that generated an energetic light that others often perceived.

Living in Naples along Florida's Gulf of Mexico, Robin reveled in the countless natural outdoor environments she could discover year-round, a distinct contrast to her former life in New York City's crowded Greenwich Village. She and Richard often spent their Sundays riding side by side on the flat open terrain marveling at the lushness of the scenery and finding sensational paths to travel.

Robin had a gutsy personality that dared to seize each experience fully and fearlessly. Even her career as a journalist had an edge as she always pushed the envelope to go deeper into stories than anyone expected, or even wanted. When she did a story about the New York City police department after they were criticized for how they handled a group of homeless people sleeping in boxes in front of Bendel's on posh 57th Street, she did ride-alongs with cops for a week, requiring a great deal of finagling. The result was an impactful story about the cops and the challenges and emotions they faced. Her stories were infused with empathy and deeper perspectives.

She turned the throttle to accelerate further along the road. She thought about the unpredictability of life. Why did she take this route instead of choosing one of the back roads this morning? Left turn can mean an amazing event. Right turn could lead to disaster. What guides us? She was pondering about why we humans make the decisions we make, when it happened.

One moment, Robin cruised cheerfully along Tamiami Trail on her way to rendezvous with Richard and his Harley Softtail and in the next moment, catastrophe. As she crossed the intersection through a green light, a white Lexus emerged from a side road clearly not stopping. In her peripheral vision, she glimpsed the vehicle and its elderly female driver approaching too rapidly. She heard ear-piercing, screeching sounds and instinctively tried to swerve out of the path. But it was too late. For Robin, the brilliant sunny day went black.

CHAPTER TWO

"*O*h, my *leetle Robeen*." Richard rolled the "R" of her name as he exaggerated his French accent in the hopes of eliciting a smile as he stood in front of Robin's gurney in the ER of the local hospital. He wore his riding clothes: tight blue jeans, a white pullover, and boots. His blue eyes were piercingly staring at her. His chiseled tanned face showed concern.

They were curtained off in a small cubicle. Bright fluorescent lights illuminated the noisy corridors filled with doctors, nurses and patients. Robin was slouched down like a child who was about to be punished, her eyes blinking open in disbelief. She wanted to disappear. Poof. Turn back the clock a few hours and start the day all over again. She felt as if her life was suddenly turned upside down literally and figuratively.

"OMG, Richard. How did I get here? How did you find out? Good God, I hurt. Do you know what happened?"

"Patience, *mon petit chou*. You got here in an ambulance. And I'm your ICE number, remember? They called me."

"My bike...?," her voice trailed off. "That...that woman...coming at me...My body...I'm so sorry, Richard. I..."

"Shhh. It's going to be okay. Your helmet saved that smart head of yours, but you've got a bad concussion. You've been unconscious for about an hour. They think your arm is broken along with a few ribs. They're going to take you to X rays shortly. But it should all be fixable. You were lucky."

"Lucky?" Robin squeaked, realizing her head would explode off her shoulders if she didn't remain still and she wondered if her neck was still in the proper position on her shoulders. Her body did not seem as if it was hers or maybe she was still too out of it from losing consciousness. The moment was surreal. It couldn't be true. But it was. "I just had an accident. Holy crap. How is that lucky? Is my bike totaled?"

"It isn't as bad as you think. From what I was told of the accident, you got hit on your back wheel, spinning your bike around which dropped to the road with you on it. You went down with the ship," he smiled comfortingly. "The Lexus continued forward and hit another car that had turned into the intersection. I think your bike can be repaired. But first you."

"Wow, is that driver ok?"

"I don't know. I came right here."

"Thanks for being here, Richard," she managed, wondering what a sight she must be with squashed helmet hair, disheveled clothes, and signs of trauma etched in her face. She thought about all the obligations she had for the week. Heck, the month. How could she be sidelined? She was too busy to have an accident.

"Good I had on my leathers, huh?" She looked down at her pants which had been torn through to her tanned skin on the left leg. "Oh my!," she exclaimed, noticing the damage.

Richard intercepted her thoughts. "They're replaceable." He patted her hand gently. "I'm so sorry I have to leave tomorrow."

"Oh no, that's right. You have that shoot in Europe. How long do you think you'll be gone?"

"It's a long one I'm afraid. We'll be in Lisbon for two weeks and then London for two weeks. I was originally thinking of adding on time to see my family, but we'll see…"

"Oh Richard, I so messed up the day."

"Shhh, it is not your fault. *C'est la vie*. Let it go."

"And my assignments…how will I get them done? My deadlines… and meetings…my life…"

"Stop, *ma cherie*. First you need to take care of you. Everything will work out."

Robin was pained, upset and red-hot anger was welling up. Why did this have to happen? And how did Richard stay so calm, so positive? Maybe because he was leaving. He wouldn't have to contend with the damage, the recovery. But it was something more in Richard. It was almost a resigned detachment from emotion. Robin could feel his compassion but at the same time, he was on a dimension removed from her frightened reality, from the catastrophe of the moment.

Maybe Richard was changed because of the family tragedy he endured. When they met, six months ago, he'd told her how much his life was impacted dramatically a year earlier when his younger sister succumbed to breast cancer, leaving behind a young son and a grieving husband. Richard had been remarkably close with his sister and was with her, holding her hand until her last breath. Richard was devastated. They always had each other's backs throughout childhood, adulthood and even when his sister began raising her own family. Above anyone in the world, Richard's sister would always be there, dependable and strong. And Richard would always be there for her, protecting her from life's evils. But cancer was an unseen enemy that snuck in and she had been in total denial. She was sure she could beat it and he believed her. He wanted to believe her. Nothing else was acceptable.

Her death gave Richard a different attitude about life and its preciousness, hitting a nerve about his own mortality. He rarely talked about his sister's illness. But he was a devoted uncle to seven-year-old Philippe, who lived with his father in Paris. Robin was sure that spending time with his family meant trying to keep his sister's memory alive and getting closer to her son, his sweet nephew.

Robin could clearly understand his wanting to be there and, of course, his work was so important. But now she wanted him here. Couldn't he stay a little longer? She needed him. Or did she? She felt conflicted by her desire for independence and not wanting to need anyone to now feeling so vulnerable, so hurt and overwhelmed by pain. Did she really want him or just the idea of having someone to care about her, to love her in her damaged state? She didn't know. She didn't know anything. She couldn't say anything to Richard about her feelings. Instead, in a reflexive nervous habit, she just wanted to check her phone. Always a distraction and an odd comfort.

"Oh my, where's my phone?"

"Unscathed. Here." He produced her phone from his pocket.

She reached for it with her right hand and grimaced in pain. "Ay, maybe broken?," she questioned. Richard leaned closer and put the phone in her seemingly unbroken left hand.

"Wow, I have quite a few messages and ironically all from Judy." Robin quickly scrolled through them. "She's asking if something's wrong."

"She got the woo-woo messages," Richard said matter-of-factly spinning his index finger in crazy-like circles next to his head.

"Oh yeah. Kinda nuts, huh? Maybe. Maybe not."

Robin and Judy had been close friends for about a decade, ever since they took a yoga training course together with a world-renowned yogi master. They bonded inextricably, like soul sisters. In the sacred space of eastern philosophies and multidimensional techniques, they both experienced personal epiphanies. They interacted on other levels. Moving from disturbances of the mind to a state of just being in the moment gave them a sensitivity to an inner space of nothingness, yet infused with an expansive awareness of everything that existed in life.

Robin, being hyper-active, found it difficult to remain on that ethereal plane but when she could, she could feel Judy vibrating at that same heightened frequency. It was as if they were meeting in a place outside of time, space, earth, or consciousness. They were both there fleetingly in an infinite world of quantum possibilities. It was simultaneously incomprehensible and immensely liberating.

Robin cherished their friendship deeply, admiring Judy's steady calmness and compassion. She felt a sister-like kinship, which helped replace her yearnings for a bond with her own sister, Jean. Jean was three years older than Robin and her polar opposite. She was ultra conservative, lacked any sense of adventure and was a homebody living in the suburbs of Long Island, childless and married to Nathan, a boring accountant. She seemed terrified to step out and take any chances. She didn't work and seemed to fill her day being a housewife, puttering around doing chores and lunching with her ladies' groups. There was nothing wrong with being a stay-at-home wife, except that she seemed to be a mere shadow of her former self and just going through the motions of living without really doing anything productive with her life.

Robin was sad just thinking about her and felt a gut-stabbing loss over the unique sisterhood she thought she once had. Family gatherings were the only time they saw one another and these would happen infrequently.

On a rare occasion, Robin would phone Jean in the hope of rekindling a connection, a glimmer of the former Jean. But the conversation was usually superficial and empty. Robin would finally end the call each time feeling a hole in her heart. Where did my real sister go? How did she turn into a Stepford wife? She wondered if perhaps she mis-remembered their childhood playfulness. Maybe Jean never was the warm, happy, loving sister. Maybe she was always the Ice Queen and Robin just imagined love between them, the joy of being together.

Growing up in their seaside community, she recalled times of biking to the park, frolicking in the surf of the Atlantic Ocean, giggling about boy crushes, consulting about first bras and school fashions, and conspiring pranks against their parents just to drive them nuts.

How did life transform her exuberant sister so totally? Or was it just in Robin's fertile imagination that had conjured up such a sister? Robin remembered her sister leaving for college, an enthusiastic bubbly teenager but that sister never came home again.

Judy's caring friendship helped fill the gaping hole left by Jean's absence and was a worthy alternative. After all, you can't pick your family, but you can pick your friends.

Judy Parkins was twin sized to Robin, same height, similar petiteness but that's where the physical similarities ended. Judy had gorgeous long-flowing blonde hair that cascaded in waves down to the middle of her back, eyes the color of swimming pools, and a perfectly featured Barbie-doll face. Robin was the opposite. She was the graceful soft shadows of chiaroscuro that gives spiciness to a black-and-white photograph. She had long, super straight cappuccino hair and lightly tanned creamy skin. She had a slight oriental appearance with high cheekbones but had absolutely no Asian heritage in her DNA.

Judy had a contagious smile that could power the lights of Times Square. She was beautiful outside and in without pretentiousness or self-absorption. She had a down to earth purity and took her powerful psychic abilities in stride.

Clearly gifted with a sixth sense, Judy had managed to dial in a special channel to Robin. She could read her mind and was able to sense her emotional signals. She is what's known as "clairsentient," capable of "feeling" and truly "knowing" when something is in discord, not with all people but most especially with Robin.

Robin stared at five different texts from Judy that had flowed onto her message queue over the last three hours. She rotated her wrist to check the time, but her watch was a broken casualty of the accident with a miserably smashed face. "Let me take that off for you," Richard offered and added, "It's just 11 a.m."

Robin's phone obeyed her command to call Judy and was immediately in voicemail. "Judy. It's Robin. I saw your concerned messages.

Anyway, you probably won't be surprised to hear I'm at the ER at Baker's. I had an accident. I think I'm okay, but you probably know better than I do. Call me when you get this. Love you."

As she ended the call, she looked sheepishly at Richard. She knew he didn't understand this extrasensory communication she had with Judy. Heck. She didn't understand it fully herself. She just knew it was special and it gave her comfort.

An hour later after a visit to radiology, Robin was back in the same cubicle only she was now alone. Richard had left on a mission to retrieve her motorcycle from wherever the police had taken it. He wanted to get it taken care of before he had to board the 7 p.m. flight out of Miami to Lisbon the next day. Robin leaned back resignedly waiting for the emergency doctor to deliver her X ray readings. She closed her eyes and sighed. Suddenly a familiar voice wafted in from the corridor.

"I'll find her." Judy was waving off a nurse and turning towards Robin's tiny space in the corner.

As Robin's eyes fluttered open, there in the flesh—not on her phone or in her imagination—was Judy with her brilliant smile.

"There's my wounded bird," Judy exclaimed, coming close to fluff up the too-thin pillow under Robin's head. "Well this is a fine mess you got yourself into this time," she kidded. "I got your voice message. Heck, didn't I warn you about staying out of hospitals? Now let's get you out of here. Where the hell is the doctor?"

Robin smiled weakly. She could smell the essential oils that Judy used in place of perfumes, sweet scents of lavender and geranium. Robin relaxed, feeling nurtured and in trusted hands.

"Thanks for coming Judy. I feel like I've been here forever."

"Let me see what I can do," Judy said in that unique gravelly voice so distinctively hers. In her hometown of Princeton, New Jersey before moving to Florida, Judy was part of the emergency room nursing staff at Princeton Community Hospital, so she knew her way around doctors, nurses, assistants, and ERs. Now living in Bonita Springs, near Naples, she owned Golden Moon, a store devoted to essential oils, gemstones, and other alternative healing products.

"Don't go anywhere," she instructed.

"Where the hell would I go?," Robin said in a pitiful tone.

Judy worked her magic and Robin was finally released by 2 p.m. with her right arm in a cast resting in a sling, her rib cage taped, and with clear instructions for managing her concussion: avoid unnecessary movements, rest, stay hydrated, and limit exposure to bright lights or loud sounds.

"No throbbing rock 'n roll music for you tonight, my little friend." Judy slowly led Robin up the indoor carpeted stairs of her condo. Robin cringed in pain with each step. Her head was pounding, her ribs hurt. She steadied slowly with each movement, sliding the hand on her "good" arm along the polished handrail. Judy cheered her enthusiastically as if she were an infant finally taking her very first tentative steps which amused Robin who was concentrating so intently on getting to the landing.

Robin was home. She cherished her bright three-bedroom condo with exposures that allowed the Naples' sunlight to flood freely into every crevice, held back only when the gauzy vanilla curtains were closed. But even then, the spacious rooms had a brilliant glow like a lightbox. Being a Piscean water sign, Robin was particularly enamored by the varied views of the fountained lake from the breakfast room off the kitchen, the living room and the bedroom, with sliding glass doors that opened from each onto a small terrace Floridians called a lanai. She often enjoyed her morning coffee watching the birds and listening to the gentle rustling of palm trees swaying in the soft breezes. Robin never thought she could feel sad in such a cheerful space. But now her inner light seemed dimmed.

Having left in a frenzied hurry that morning since she never liked being late, especially when meeting Richard, she surveyed the dishes left on the sink, from a quick coffee and half-eaten bagel. The weather channel was still blaring on the TV in the living room and her bed was a tangled mess of linens. Judy straightened the sheets and comforter, puffed up the pillows and settled Robin comfortably, opening the curtains to a clear view of the lake

"Well that was exhausting," Robin sighed. "What a wreck I am. Let's see, three broken ribs, a broken arm and a concussion. I feel like crap."

Judy suggested she get some rest. She fixed a small tray of toast and a protein drink along with a glass of water and bottle of pain pills, suggesting she take another one around dinner time.

"You really want to stay ahead of the pain," directed Judy.

"Roger that," Robin said in a weak voice.

Judy had to get back to the store, but she'd check on her later. She kissed the air in front of Robin's forehead.

"I can see how chaotic your aura is right now. Trauma will do that. So, do deep breathing as you're able. It'll calm your nervous system. And stop those damn thoughts. This was not your fault."

Judy nodded in acceptance. The uncanny ability Judy possessed to "read" Robin both unnerved and delighted her. A bizarre phenomenon reminiscent of what she once had with her mother.

Of course, many moms have strong maternal instincts that allow them to know when their child needs them, no matter what age. But the mystical connection Robin had with her mother was mega dimensions beyond that. It was more like her mother could read her precise thoughts in little bubbles floating above her head. And it didn't matter if she was across a room or on the other side of the city. She could always feel on a deep visceral level what Robin was contemplating and she had a precognitive intuition of exactly what was going to happen. In all the instances that Robin was aware of in which her mother tuned in, her predictions were eerily accurate. Robin felt both unsettled and comforted by her mother's intuition. Often her mother tried to suppress her psychic senses so as not to trespass on her daughter's privacy or freak her out. But it was always there lurking in the background like a hungry tiger staging to pounce.

And then suddenly that distinctive reliable ability disappeared, along with her mother.

CHAPTER THREE

MAY 1994

*R*obin was just about to turn 20, completing her junior year at New York University. To finalize her degree, she was resigned to having to attend summer school. Her parents had been disapproving of the extension, especially her mother. But Robin had changed her major too many times and she was short on credits needed to graduate.

Another contribution to this deficiency was that Robin had taken a semester at the University of California at Los Angeles only to find out that only half those courses were recognized by NYU. Again, her mother was dismayed that Robin hadn't researched the situation better.

Her mother–who the world knew as Ruth Stevens–was always practical, logical and frugal. She didn't understand why Robin wanted to travel to UCLA on the other side of the country when she was already productively enrolled in a quality university. They had debated for weeks but Robin was unrelenting and finally her mother had agreed to let her make her own mistakes. Even though Robin was unfortunately having to pay the consequences with a harder course load, her mother never uttered a single guilt-producing "I told you so." Of course, she didn't have to. Robin knew her mother had seen the outcome of Robin's bad choices in her uncanny psychic way. She wished now that she had heeded her mother's warnings more closely but there was no going back. Finally, by next fall, she would reach the finish line with a degree in journalism.

Fortunately, Robin was already getting a few story assignments from editors she had met through various professors, a fact that made her feel proud. She enjoyed knowing how her mother's face would light up when she told her about the newest article she was working on. Even though she didn't get paid much, she was carving her path. Her mother was always supportive and seemed enthused.

Now that she was moving into the adult work world, Robin was becoming closer to her mom. She'd phone her often to chat about things that were going on. Robin wanted independence while still desperately seeking her mother's approval. She was becoming more attached to truly hearing her mother's wisdom and perspective. In fact, she was increasingly leaning on her for advice on everything from the way she wore her hair to guys she was dating to assignments to accept or reject. Robin was starting to trust her mother's special powers more and more each day. And she enjoyed hearing updates about her mother's plans for her annual girlfriends' getaway trip that was coming up soon.

While her semester at UCLA had taken her off the beaten path, Robin found enjoyment in her brief experience in Westwood's Los Angeles. But clearly, living in New York City's Greenwich Village was the ultimate thrill.

A devoted people watcher, Robin enjoyed observing streets filled with a mix of students, musicians, artists, and regular average working New Yorkers. The city was pulsing with non-stop activity and the tempting promise of discovery. A favorite pastime was a stroll down Greenwich Avenue to the antique consignment shop where she'd find cool, trendy capes or jackets at exceptionally low prices. Bleecker Street was another attraction for pizza, ice cream or window shopping. And she adored installing herself at the outdoor seating of the Riviera Café, weather permitting, on the busy corner of West 4th Street and 7th Avenue. Masses of strangers passing by on the street always seemed in a hurry. They had somewhere important to go, something urgent to do. Fast walking to a meeting, a performance, a gallery opening, a dinner rendezvous, a class, an appointment, or even just pushing a stroller. A melting pot of possibilities. The Village had a unique pace, creatively its own. Robin felt invisible as she took in the scene. She was inhaling all the moments, but no one could really see her in the blur of city life, like an indistinct but suggestive impressionist painting. She was there as a form of colors, atoms congealing together in some unfocused physical mass.

She both loved and hated the city. At times, she felt overwhelmed by the crowds, the smells of garbage and car fumes, the traffic, honking horns, ambulance sirens. These were all mind-numbing assaults on her senses. The worst confrontations were the sad-looking homeless people begging for money or food.

From her early days when she rented a tiny studio apartment across from the entrance to Gansevoort Street, she resolved not to engage with these so called "bums" and not to give anything, not money and not even a glance. It was the only way she could avoid the heart-wrenching decision with each encounter as to whether to give or not to give, not that she had much money as a student. But she was distraught at seeing their plight and was forced to devise a survival mechanism to deflect those disturbing feelings. Putting on mental blinders did the trick and she soon realized why so many New Yorkers developed that steely, cold, blank exterior. It was the only way to navigate all the slings and arrows flying around in the Big Apple. The nastiness could pierce you, take you by surprise, and cause harm. She was intent on appreciating the good parts of the city and ignored the bad, almost as if the icky stuff would dissolve into nothingness if she paid it no attention.

She lived alone and adored the location of her apartment which was walkable to everywhere in the village, even though it was on the edge of the rat-infested meat-packing district. If she awoke in the middle of the night, she'd flick on the kitchen light with her eyes closed until the sounds of scattering roaches stopped. She deluded herself into believing if she didn't see them, she wouldn't scream. It didn't always work. But it was her little private piece of New York. Albeit a little creepy, it was affordable. Years later, the area would become chic and much more expensive when the elevated park and High Line promenade was built on an abandoned freight rail line just a block north. Her street would be transformed, dotted with high-end clothing boutiques and trendy cafés. But she was long gone by then.

Her studio with the charming red brick wall and working fireplace as its only desirable features wasn't even the square footage of the bedroom she had shared with her sister growing up. To make the most of the space, she had thought she was superbly inventive by ordering a Murphy bed, arguing with the installer to put it vertically against the wall rather than taking up so much wall space horizontally. After all, she had artwork she wanted to display and with one wall consumed by bricks, there weren't many surfaces available.

The workman had vehemently protested, complaining that the bed might not work as well and the design was constructed to provide ample room for a desk when it was closed against the wall, an item that could be added to her order. In her creative defiance, she demanded the bed be installed her way. But as it turned out, the well-built wooden frame with extra storage proved to be quite heavy to lift into place each night as the massive spring strained to manage the vertically extended weight load. And then right at the beginning of a holiday weekend, the whole damn bed heaved away from its enormous steel coil and bolt construction and launched itself immovably sideways into the middle of her already small space. She had had to live with no bed and an awkward oak tank-like piece of furniture taking up most of her apartment until Monday when she had to sheepishly admit to the store owner that his installer had been right. She needed help as soon as possible. His response was foul and unsympathetic. He could send someone on Wednesday. Robin was unprepared for such dismissive treatment.

Growing up in a small beach-front community outside the city had protected Robin from the darkness of crime, misfortune, and pain. Her formative years were spent in a town that was friendly, safe where people were neighborly and cooperative. She could never quite adjust to New York's abrasiveness. None of that happened in her town, except once.

She vividly remembered one summer afternoon that broke the peace and quiet. People were streaming by her house on their way from the beach late in the afternoon. She was outdoors keeping her dad company at the grill in the driveway while he busily barbecued chicken along with his special potato medley with onions and green peppers, seasoned with lots of salt and pepper.

The Stevens family was having their typical Sunday BBQ joined by a couple of adult cousins who had come to lounge on the beach for the day. It was just Robin and her dad outside when all at once they heard a loud "crack" and then another "crack," which echoed loudly through the street. They wondered about those odd sounds but the meal was ready to be taken inside to the others who were joyously playing music together in the living room. Guitars, accordions and a trumpet were all blending their lively notes in a loud cacophony of joy and fun. None of them heard the sirens.

After dinner, the neighbor, Mr. Philips, came pounding on the front door to see if they'd heard what happened to Dara. Hardly stopping to catch his breath, Mr. Philips related the shocking story about the strikingly beautiful 19-year-old Dara, the daughter of another neighbor, who was shot at point blank range by her jealous 20-year-old boyfriend because she was leaving him. And then he shot himself. Robin was nine years old and it made an indelible impression, especially the next morning when she saw a pool of blood in the street where she waited for the bus to school. Her stomach did flip flops and for months she had nightmares.

Mostly Robin had lived a carefree middle-class existence and city life was sometimes debilitating for a compassionate, sensitive person like her. Tragedies happened all the time, 24/7. Her nature was always to help others in any way humanly possible. But the streets of the Village were filled with people she could never benefit. She was better off not seeing those realities, to be more like the Hansom cab horses around Central Park with leather blinders on their bridles blocking their eyes from getting spooked by distractions.

On the last day of the semester, a Tuesday afternoon in mid-May, Robin was hurriedly passing through the main room of NYU's student center, admiring the views of Washington Square Park through expansive windows flooding spring sunshine into the sprawling room of couches and meeting areas. Suddenly, a fellow student frantically shouted her name.

She knew the student, Matt, a wiry, nerdy guy who was always jumpy and awkward. He was at the bank of phones, cradling one off its hook. "Robin, Robin, you have a call. Your sister. She says it's urgent."

If Jean is calling me, Robin thought, pigs must be flying over the Empire State Building. She abruptly grabbed the phone out of Matt's waving hand.

"Jean?," she said tentatively into the phone. Her sister was sobbing uncontrollably. Now with alarm in her voice, "Jean, what is it? What's wrong?"

Between gasps for air, Jean choked out the words, "It's mom. She's gone."

"WHAT???," Robin barked in confusion. "What do you mean gone? Gone on her trip?"

"No… I mean, yes, but…they can't find her."

"What the hell is going on?"

"I don't know. I don't know," Jean said as she sucked in big gulps of air. "She vanished. Thin air. Gone."

"What the hell are you saying? Mom just disappeared?"

"Yes. Yes." Jean cried even louder, so loud that Robin put her hand to muffle the speaker so the overwhelming vibrations emanating from the phone wouldn't collapse the whole wall of phones. "Call dad. It's just awful." And with that, Jean hung up.

Robin glanced out to the park, not seeing the dog walkers or the students racing across the grassy areas to their classes or the old guys playing chess at the cemented chess boards. All she saw was… nothing. She felt nothing. Void of feeling, she was numb with shock.

She picked the phone back off its cradle and dialed her parents' number. Her father answered on the second ring. "Hello," he said, his voice hoarse and strained. "Dad, what's going on? Jean just called me. Where's mom?"

"Hi Peaches," he said with both warmth and sadness. "Can you come home right away? We need you here."

"Of course, daddy. What's happened?"

"Just come home as soon as you can," he said, and the phone went dead.

CHAPTER FOUR

MAY 1994

*R*uth Stevens was ecstatic to be traveling once again with her two childhood friends on their annual girls' getaway.

They named themselves the "Triple Ts" for Titillating Troublemaking Trio, since they seemed to encourage one another to live these trips in some fantasy fugue that whisked them far from their husbands and children for the week. They had only missed one year because Nan was having her second child Luke, the same year that Stephanie had to take care of her ailing mother-in-law, whose body succumbed within months to colon cancer at 63. The women stayed in touch through it all, to share life's polarities of birth and death, good news, and sad news. Even though physically separated, they leaned on one another emotionally, understanding and supporting each other's journeys.

This was the official 25th anniversary year of their getaways. Now in their mid-40s, they agreed on a trip outside North America to the South of France, particularly auspicious as they extended their once-in-a-lifetime excursion to two full weeks. This was way outside the norm.

As their plane touched down at the Nice airport, the women were consumed by an innocent giddiness. They had arranged for a rental car to drive to Arles for their stay in Provence. As they peered through the plane's window expectantly, they were greeted by a runway bathed in bright sunshine and an azure sky dotted with puffy white clouds.

"On arrive," announced Nan, shaking her long blonde hair free of her *barrette*. Her crystal blue eyes sparkled with light despite tiredness from jet lag. Childbirth and motherhood had thickened her once svelte figure, but she still could turn heads both male and female with her smart, stylish look. At 5'9" she made a commanding impression. She wore a soft pink, comfortably loose dress adorned with a lavish paisley scarf that she now draped around her bare shoulders to keep away the draftiness of the plane. She was the only one of the friends who spoke any French.

"Looks like a gorgeous day," said Ruth, who in contrast had a slight build and sported a short dark brown pixie haircut framing her perfect skin and dancing light brown eyes. She had an impish yet mesmerizing countenance and even after birthing two daughters, had retained a trim, youthful body which she had clothed in blue jeans and a long-sleeved white button-down shirt, cinched fashionably with a large chain link silver belt.

Stephanie marched to the beat of a vastly different loud Congo drummer, with a distinctly unique personality. She carried about 35 unneeded pounds on her 5'3" frame and had a sloppy yet artsy way of dressing. Today she wore an oversized African print blouse over stretchy pants, which she insisted on demonstrating just how very stretchy they were when they first boarded the plane at New York's JFK airport. She lifted her blouse and kept snapping the elastic waistband against her fleshy belly to the amusement of boarding passengers. She was boisterous, funny, and refused to take herself too seriously.

Notoriously incapable of traveling light, they piled themselves and their copious luggage into a 4-door silver Citroen. Ruth was proudly at the wheel, recalling *The Day of the Jackal*.

"Don't you remember the assassination attempt on Charles de Gaulle? He credited his survival on a Citroen"

"Really? How's that?" Stephanie wondered.

"Yeah, his motorcade was ambushed, and the car and all its tires were riddled with machine gun bullets and yet the car still went at full speed. Saved his life."

"Cheers for the car," Nan chimed in.

"I'm just saying what a safe car this is," Ruth added.

"You mean if we're attacked by a mob?," Stephanie quipped.

"Hey, you never know what can happen," Ruth asserted with playful sarcasm.

They all laughed.

"I should ask if you're feeling threatened or unsafe," said Nan, unfolding a map to plot their route.

Ruth assured Nan there was no need to pull out her psychological mumbo jumbo on her.

"I just need you to tell me where to go," Ruth told Nan with a smirk.

"Is that figuratively or literally?" Nan teased and began to call out directions to continue straight onto Route de Grenoble. Then left onto the A8 ramp to Marseille/Cannes/Antibes. Then the E80/A54 exit towards Arles/Nimes.

"It's about 250 kilometers. Should take two-and-a-half hours unless we want to stop along the way," said Nan.

"Like in Cannes?," asked Stephanie suggestively.

"I take it you want to stop there," Ruth said with a big smile. The Triple Ts always exhibited a cooperative rapport, devoid of egocentric conflicts. Ebbing and flowing with everyone's requests made their friendship seamless and pleasurable. They were excellent travel mates.

Without any further discussion, they decided on a late lunch in Cannes as a perfect kick-start to their *sejour.*

As they drove, they shared small talk about their families. Since they each had married and scattered to different states, they rarely got together *en famille*. Sure, they spoke by phone but not very often as their circles were separate and their own responsibilities absorbed their days. They had grown up together in an immigrant-filled community in Brooklyn, near the famous Coney Island amusement park, but after high school they followed dissimilar paths.

Ruth met Teddy in her sophomore year at Brooklyn College. He was a shy graduate student working part time in his father's warehouse business. But even with his tentativeness, he fell madly for Ruth and came thundering out of his shell, taking her into the back seat of his rundown old red Mustang on their tenth date, getting her pregnant and forcing a shotgun wedding. Ruth had aspired to become a legal assistant or even a full-fledged attorney. She loved learning and was smart academically, always at the top of her class, but she never finished her degree.

She was smitten by Teddy, but the dramatic turn of events somehow caused her to lose control of her life. She was not convinced she wanted to get married nor become the mother of Teddy's child at only 19 years old. But it was too late. She was Teddy's wife and about to be a mother. This shift in her expectations made her feel as if she were on the sidelines of her own life. She was going through the motions of living but somehow had become a bystander, unemotionally watching as she and Teddy coupled and brought Jean into the world. Ruth threw herself into motherhood but there was always a deep-seated yearning for a different kind of life and niggling thoughts that questioned "what if" she hadn't gotten pregnant. The uncertainties were pushed deep into the marrow of her bones and hidden so fully that she never uttered a word about life's dissatisfactions to anyone, always trying to find ways to fix things on her own.

Providing for his new family, Teddy went to work full time in his father's business in Long Island City, the factory center of Queens that afforded the newlywed parents a modest bungalow in a lovely beach town 45 minutes from Manhattan. It was a quiet community with good schools where they could peacefully raise their little one.

Occasionally Ruth helped by doing secretarial work that Teddy brought home to her, mostly organizing files and some accounting. Otherwise, she spent her days keeping their home immaculate and reading books. She especially enjoyed biographies, which allowed her to be a voyeur into someone else's life, and when she would choose a woman's story of accomplishment and adventure, she would imagine she was that exciting woman. She was enthralled by Marie Curie, Anaïs Nin, Zelda Fitzgerald, and enjoyed stories about Amelia Earhart or modern celebrities like Candice Bergen, Cher, or Jane Fonda.

Stories became her escape from her suburban, lackluster existence. She would disappear so fully into the pages that if her ceiling would have collapsed on her, she would not have noticed, which actually happened once. Well, not really collapsed but it dripped water from an overflowing bathtub that seven-year-old Jean had forgotten to mind and ended up causing costly repairs and a severe punishment of a 30-day ban on television. "If she couldn't watch the bathwater filling, she should not have the privilege of watching her favorite programs," was Teddy's strict rationale. By that time their second daughter, Robin, was already four years old.

Stephanie Waters met her husband, Steve, in the art supply store in which he was part owner. It was located near Parsons School of Design at the New School in lower Manhattan where Stephanie waffled between a degree in communication design and fine arts.

She was so drawn to explore the artist's tools of the trade that Steve's store became the center of her attention. Instead of hanging out at a coffee shop by day or a bar by night, Stephanie's greatest joy was trolling the aisles ogling the colors of pastels, choosing a special brush for her latest oil painting or snagging a set of calligraphy pens on sale.

A throwback to the long-ago hippie days of the sixties, Stephanie embodied the laid-back style and attitude of that earlier time and Steve found her fascinating. Steve and his business partner expanded, opening stores in New Brunswick and Princeton, New Jersey. Their flagship store opened at the Princeton Shopping Center about the same time Steve proposed to Stephanie and they settled in a small brick-faced home on the countrified outskirts of Princeton where Stephanie found great inspiration to continue her landscape paintings.

Nan began chatting about how quickly Luke is catching up to his big brother both academically and athletically. "He's only 11 but he's already Jonathan's height. He's a damn weed. I swear from the time he gets on the school bus to the time he comes home, his pants look like they've shrunk. He's like bamboo. I can't keep up with his growth spurts."

Laughter filled the interior of the super comfortable car as they cruised along the toll road, with Nan riding shotgun and Stephanie sprawled in the back seat.

Nan Peters was the only Ivy-leaguer of the three, having attended Harvard College. Her education began in liberal arts without a serious major until her second year when she had the good fortune to take a class with Dr. Herbert Benson. Dr. Benson invented the term "relaxation response" about meditation and the body's ability to stimulate the relaxation of muscle and organs. He was a professor of mind-body medicine and a founding trustee of The American Institute of Stress.

Studying with Dr. Benson, Nan became fascinated by the field of psychology and how human behavior influences biology. After graduation, she wrote a fairly well-received book called *Letting Go of Stress* and began a small therapy practice in Cambridge. Nan met George at a book signing at Barnes & Noble as he had just authored a book about how looking your best influences how to feel your best. He was witty, tall, handsome...and a doctor. They were married a year later, and George guided them to Stamford, Connecticut where he had grown up and where he opened his own surgery center focused on beautification through facelifts, rhinoplasties and other plastic surgeries.

While Nan possessed more of a decided sophistication than her friends and lived in affluence with her surgeon husband, she never lauded her academic or economic advantages over her girlfriends. They were all one and the same, from the same roots, and she believed in friendship without strings. She considered their sisterhood beyond special; it resonated at the very core of their being. Their essences were intertwined forever.

"My kid didn't fall far from the tree," announced Stephanie, after the laughter about Nan's bamboo-growing son subsided. "Sarah's going to be an *artiste* like her mom. I'm so proud of her. She won a scholarship to Parsons and starts in September."

Nan and Ruth extended hearty congratulations, speaking over each other in their enthusiasm to support the exciting news. Stephanie and Steve doted on Sarah. The moon and the stars revolved around her, almost too much. Ruth silently wondered if someone can be smothered by too much love and attention. If so, Sarah would be a perfect candidate. She doubted they would handle empty nesting very well.

No one said another word until Ruth decided it must be her turn, so she shared about her oldest daughter living with husband Nathan, the successful accountant on Long Island. Jean seemed to be doing well, but there was remorse in Ruth's tone.

"Jean still has no kids," she confessed in a voice that clearly revealed disappointment. "I thought maybe she'd adopt."

Nan instantly reacted to Ruth's tone by counseling her about how important it is to accept the choices of grown kids and to let go of expectations. "They need to know we love them without trappings. And it isn't healthy to project our needs or wishes onto them or we harm them and ourselves. This is their journey. We can only plant the seeds and values and then…"

Nan paused, realizing her words were landing like a damper on everyone. "Sorry. I'm really going to be on vacation now." She twisted her fingers in front of her puckered lips as if locking them with an invisible key.

Ruth smiled and mentioned Robin, who was just about to graduate from NYU with a degree in journalism, adding that she'd probably stay in the city with all the publishing opportunities there. Ruth beamed that she'd already gotten a couple of freelance assignments.

"In fact, next week she's got a plum interview with that wild, famous photographer Peter Beard. He has an exhibition at the International Center of Photography and Robin is doing a story for a small art magazine." She paused.

Stephanie was the first to respond with boundless keenness. "Oh my gosh, he's dreamy. He did all those death-defying photographs of African wildlife. I'm jealous. I want to read that story."

"I'll make sure you get a copy," Ruth assured.

"Okay, ladies, as exciting as all the family news is, that's enough homey talk. We're in friggin' France together." Stephanie spewed spittle with her exuberant delivery. They all agreed to spend less time focused on what they've decided to take a break from, their real lives, and more time engaged fully and completely in this dream vacation they've made happen.

"I'm still pinching myself that we're really here together," said Ruth.

They all nodded, acknowledging how amazing it was to have pulled off a two-week time-out from everyday life, including from their spouses. Ruth commented how refreshing vacations are and admitted that she felt a little stuck in her daily routines. She was looking for a new perspective and the wherewithal to change the humdrum. "Add more sparkle," she said with a clicking of her tongue as if coaxing a horse to gallop faster.

"I'm not getting any younger," said Ruth with a flourish as if articulating this sentiment for all of them.

They bickered about whether middle age is old. They decided it depends on your vantage point. If you're 11-year-old Luke, 45 is ancient whereas someone who is 85 might think they were just hitting their stride and would urge them not to squander this time. And yet their age had its challenges.

Nan discussed research that showed life satisfaction follows a "Happiness U-Curve," dropping to its lowest point in midlife and shifting upwards around age 50. This paradox of aging follows a major happiness slump around age 43.

"Oh gosh, that's us," said Stephanie. "We've got kids on one end and elderly parents on the other sandwiching us in STRESS."

"And the dread of aging, getting incapacitated. Ugh," Ruth commented.

"Agree," said Nan, explaining that the study revealed that life satisfaction improves as fear of aging gives way to savoring and appreciating and a recognition that life is, after all, fleeting. As theologian John Calvin understood in the 16th century, "Here today, gone tomorrow."

Nan laughed. "Oddly enough, this bizarre happiness curve is replicated in chimps and orangutans."

"What?" Stephanie shook her head.

"Really. A study group at the University of Edinburgh in Scotland enlisted longtime handlers of more than 500 animals at zoos in five countries to report on specific findings. They were asked to fill out a questionnaire about the well-being of these animals, especially their mood and enjoyment of social interactions. The results are conclusive, suggesting that perhaps there is a biological component to this slump." Nan giggled at the notion and the car rocked with laugher.

"So that gives us reason to look forward to being 50, huh?" Ruth piped in, still cackling loudly.

Ensconced at last in the Café Pico in a historic area on Avenue du Pecaud, just two steps to the Plage du Midi, they placed their orders with Nan's able assistance. The atmosphere was friendly, and the plates were quickly delivered. They were tickled to be lunching in the famous French Riviera destination of Cannes.

Stephanie surveyed her *Hamburger Americain* and *pommes frites* with curiosity, as it hardly resembled what she expected. The coarsely chopped meat patty has some green particles mashed in and was on a bigger-than-mouth-sized French baguette. She squashed the height with her hand and ventured a bite. Pleased with her mixed salad and assorted cheese plate, Nan commented on the way the white silky Camembert cheese seeped out onto the plate like lava from a volcano. Stephanie jumped on the observation, reminded of how Camembert, or maybe it was Brie, had served as inspiration for the oozing clock draped over a barren tree branch in Salvador Dali's famous painting, *Persistence of Memory.*

"I'm determined to taste as many of the 400 cheese varieties that I can before the end of our trip," Nan announced. "Although I know there are a few that are only ripe at a certain time of year and if you eat it outside of its readiness, it's actually poison to your system."

Stephanie retorted, "Well that doesn't sound worth the risk!"

"Yum," exclaimed Ruth after the first tantalizing bite of her *Croque Monsieur,* a hot sandwich made with ham and Gruyere cheese. "Would be nice to have a glass of wine but I'm afraid it would put me to sleep." They all agreed and instead shared a large pitcher of sparkling water. None of them had realized how hungry they were as conversations took a momentary hiatus.

After lunch, they decided to stroll the sandy beach of the Cote D'Azur and gaze out at the Mediterranean Sea. How could they come to Cannes and not see the famous beaches? Pinpoints of reflected light danced across the deep blue undulating surface of the sea, like star constellations. The scene was breathtaking and awe-inspiring. A thin promenade along the back of the beach was peppered with cyclists and joggers. The stretch of sandy shoreline was filled with colorful umbrellas and lounge chairs, populated by bikini clad nymphs and buff-looking Frenchmen. The three women stood absolutely motionless, scanning the sights in admiration, imagining the glamorous movie stars and celebrities who flocked here for the famous annual film festival which had just ended the previous week.

"What are you doing?," Nan called after Stephanie, who slipped off her sneakers and socks and was hustling toward the water's edge.

"Be right back," she yelled back. "I've got to get my tootsies in there." And with that, her colorful mass of earth-toned African patterns flew in the breeze next to toned, bathing-suited beauties.

"Wow, that was a worthwhile stop." Ruth was back behind the wheel with Nan barking directions and Stephanie being a back-seat driver.

"Next stop Arles," said Nan.

"Remind me again why we picked Arles?" Stephanie queried.

Ruth reminded them of the book that had inspired them.

"Remember reading *A Year in Provence*?," Ruth asked, waiting for Stephanie's vague 'uh huh' with urgings for Ruth to continue.

"We decided Aix en Provence was too touristy. Arles seemed more interesting and less traveled."

"And besides, one of my neighbors told me it's an amazing place," Ruth declared. "He attends the annual photography festival, the *Rencontres Internationales de la Photographie* and last year he actually presented a session on American photography. He's the one who recommended the Grand Hôtel Pinus-Nord," she added, tripping over the pronunciation which came out "penis."

Stephanie didn't miss a beat. "Oh yeah. That's where three middle-aged married women should stay. For sure!"

Bursts of uncontrollable laughter erupted.

"Okay, so listen up," demanded Ruth. "He told me about the history, how during the late Roman Empire, Arles became a renowned cultural and religious center and lots of Roman remnants still exist. It's on the Rhone and has the largest wetlands in France, the Camargue. The sunlight is supposed to be amazing and it's attracted many artists like Van Gogh."

"Well, get ready Arles. Here come the Triple Ts," joked Stephanie.

*T*he neon red glare of numbers floating on the nightstand taunted

FEBRUARY 2019

Robin as she squinted to see that the time was 3:30 a.m. Another sleepless night. A moment before, she had finally entered a blissful non-thinking space but now her thoughts came thundering back, along with the pain. Had she been stupid in the way she lived? She pushed away the emptiness she felt and gently wriggled her body in search of a more comfortable position. Lost and hopeless, she hurt everywhere.

Lying in her warm bed in agonizing pain, Robin felt consumed by questions. Maybe my friends are right. Maybe I'm too old for these daring adventures. Maybe I need to act my age. Sell my motorcycle.

The mere thoughts made her stomach ache. She didn't know what acting her age looked like and she knew she didn't want to. Yet pain and vulnerability were weakening her spirit. She'd thought she was a strong independent woman. Or had that been just a facade? A masquerade of who she thought she should be? Wanted to be? Sad sack of broken bones was more appropriate now. What motivated her to seek dangerous experiences without considering the consequences?

A shy and withdrawn child, Robin's personality changed drastically after her mother disappeared from her life. Suddenly an inner beast emerged, a strange creature who indulged in risky behaviors with a careless, cavalier attitude. Before then, she had felt safe and protected. Ruth had been her north star, her guiding light. Without her mother's influence and presence, Robin was misplaced and abandoned. Devoid of feeling, she didn't belong anywhere. Roller coasters, motorcycles, careless relationships, and dangerous escapades provided a rush of sensations. Nothing lasted, but became temporary reminders that Robin was alive. The wounds in her heart, the nothingness, were camouflaged by busy schedules and constant activities that left little time to ponder the inner anguish. The dark hidden questions that lurked within her never got answered: was her mother alive and would she ever feel loved again?

Like her mother, she had an insatiably curious mind and always wanted to see around the next corner, learn the next insight. Or was it that she just disliked being "normal," not wanting to be part of the pack or robotically following what her peers thought they "should" be doing? Never wanting to settle for ordinary, Robin continually blazed fresh paths, but she seemed to do so with mindless abandon. And now she was grounded. What would she do? What's next?

Being a freelance writer gave her expansive opportunities to snag assignments that allowed her to explore her peculiar interests. Of course, some of her pursuits barely paid the bills, such as the two-month cross-country trip on her motorcycle. She was doing a story for a lifestyle magazine and set out on her Harley with a platonic friend Barry on his stable Honda Goldwing. Barry was the perfect friend to travel with as there was no temptation of engaging in any kind of relationship beyond sharing an extraordinary ride. Barry was extremely attractive and sturdy but decidedly gay. He and Robin had a smooth, fun banter between them and a clear respect for one another's space, accepting each other's sexuality. They shared a desire to seek nuggets of life and search for meaning. Or was it a search for love?

It was a year ago in early June when they embarked on their 12,000-mile tour meandering from New York City through the Midwest, up to the Canadian Rockies, out to California and even across Vancouver on a ferry to Victoria Island. To save money, they pitched a tent at campsites and cooked food over a campfire. But they soon discovered the soaking morning dew made packing their camping equipment impossible. This prolonged their departure to almost noon giving them an extremely late start on the road. So, they resorted to staying in cheap motels and eating at inexpensive diners.

The trip was eye-opening and gave Robin a unique look at North America, its awe-inspiring landscapes and people of all races and status from farmers to fellow travelers. She found a different kind of love for the land and all the people trying to make their way through life and carving their reality from a tiny slice of the world. But as the trip ended, returning to the city, she was worn out from such a nomadic existence for over 60 days. She peered closer at her own reality in a tiny box in a New York apartment building. What was important? What did she value? For the moment, sleeping in her own bed was a luxury she relished. She'd think about it in the morning.

Though not beautiful in a classic way, Robin was strikingly attractive. She had a sexual appeal to the opposite sex. Her long, lustrous chestnut locks framed a heart-shaped face with luminous golden-brown eyes. She maintained her fitness, resulting in a lean and curved figure. Wherever she went, she drew attention. Riding into town on her motorcycle with all her protective garb, she still looked too young and too tiny to be doing what she was doing, especially back in her early twenties. She looked younger than her chronological age and was carded at bars well into her late thirties. Although slight of stature, she had an enormous heart that smiled through in her animated, enthusiastic style. When she entered a room, she brought a buoyant glow that lit up the space and became a magnetic draw. She possessed a special energy that others unconsciously admired. She clearly had a fierce independence, a seemingly carefree zest for living which was contagious.

A study in contrast, Robin's high-energy, confident exterior was in conflict with her immense shyness and insecurity, a throwback to her childhood and her loss of direction. Few knew her fears and anxieties. Large social gatherings made her uncomfortable as she believed she was incapable of making small talk. She envied those social butterflies who could flit seamlessly from person to person, discussing mostly inconsequential topics. She felt safer in smaller circles.

She didn't want to be judged for her lofty ideas about life. She had an insatiable desire to understand her purpose, and seriously wanted to know everyone else's. Why are we here? We're born. We live. We die. What did it mean? The dash. Chatting about the weather or the latest gossip, standing over high tables with wine glasses constantly being refilled, was never her bailiwick. She preferred one-on-one conversations with a few close friends, exploring inner secrets of life and its fleetingness.

Her earliest recollection of life's transience was when she was just six years old. She'd walked the half block to her house from the school bus. As soon as she entered, her sister Jean angrily screamed at her that their parakeet was dead, and it was Robin's fault. Robin was responsible for feeding the pretty bird who had very striking green, yellow and orange markings, Jean insisted that their pet died of starvation. Robin teared up and sulked off to the kitchen to have her after school snack of chocolate milk and Oreo cookies alone at the small table.

Suddenly Robin had a realization that the little bird was gone forever and that one day Robin would be gone, too. The concept of death, the notion of not existing, not being in her body, not seeing her parents or friends terrified her. She would become nothing, thrown into the trash like her feathered pet and discarded. Her stomach twisted into inner gymnastics. She pushed her chair back from the table as if the motion would halt her unsettling thoughts. Just then her mother entered the room. Seeing a panicked expression on Robin's tear-filled face, her mom asked, "Is something wrong, little one"? But Robin couldn't talk. She just sobbed.

Robin chose to do everything off the beaten path, never following classic guidance or the wisdom of experience. She trusted an inner GPS that led her to unique insights, but only when all the stars aligned, which wasn't that often. Her accident was a perfect example of its failure. She hadn't slept well the night before and should have asked Richard for a raincheck. Her reflexes were compromised, and she shouldn't have been on her bike that fateful morning. She was haunted by a history of poor choices and forgiving herself was impossible. She'd been stupid.

Confined to bed popping pain pills, Robin struggled, feeling totally challenged by life and crushingly lonely. Richard had left for his modeling assignment and her friends were understandably busy with their lives. Time seemed to be moving at a snail's pace and she couldn't help thinking she would never be herself again. She would never be pain-free or heal. Not only was her body broken in multiple places, so was her spirit. It was as if air that was supposed to fill her soul like an inflatable balloon had been punctured and gravity-defying oxygen had escaped, leaked out and abandoned her, dropping her with a thud in a dark depressing suffocating underground.

She pondered half aloud, "With my one wing clipped, maybe I'm no longer the free bird, no longer living up to my name. Maybe I need to grow up and reassess my choices in life." Her body was crying out for attention and care.

Suddenly Robin let out a surprised gasp as her friend Suzanne appeared out of thin air at the foot of the bed.

"Can anyone join this pity party or is it private?," she asked jokingly. "Sorry didn't mean to startle you."

Suzanne had let herself in through the front door as Robin had instructed. A science writer from Robin's freelance days in New York, Suzanne was a few years older and had become a successful entrepreneur in Naples, designing and creating several lines of comfortable women's golf casuals.

Back in their city days, the friends' closets were filled with monochromatic clothes of black, brown or navy, the accepted city uniform. But Florida brought out vibrance and a delightful range of colors. Like many who relocate to this tropical jewel along the

Gulf of Mexico, Suzanne had shed her northern trappings like an unnecessary winter coat. A different part of her emerged as she uncovered aspects of herself, she never had the time or inclination to find before moving here. Who knew she was a designer? Certainly, she hadn't a clue, but there was something inspirational about where she lived, its proximity to nature, wildlife, waterways, abundant sunshine. It stimulated a response of gratitude every day.

Instead of the dirty browning snows of winter or the granite grays and darkness of the northern terrain or the unbearable crowds, all Suzanne's senses were titillated by the warm blossoming of greens, blues, florals and even the full spectrum of double rainbows which seemed like nature's most impressive gift. And just like that, she began working with a local clothing manufacturer creating spectacularly beautiful and comfortable fashion lines for women golfers, of which there were many in Southwest Florida.

Like Judy, Suzanne was part of Robin's inner circle, the only other person Robin truly felt lived up to being a genuine friend, someone who made her a better person just through non-judgmental support and caring. They had been through a lot together over the years and both cherished their closeness and admired one another.

Robin was thrilled when Suzanne moved to Naples and was even more enamored with her gutsiness in starting a business, a huge deviation from the days of writing about science and technology. Robin was always encouraging, offering both emotional and artistic feedback and Suzanne's business was now flourishing as her designs were selling all over the country, especially in golf resorts.

Today Suzanne wore one of her outfits from the watercolor pastel line, a pale blue, round-necked, sleeveless shirt with white knee-length shorts that had little matching pale blue diamond shapes on each side seam. It was a crisp, tidy look. She wore her long auburn hair pulled tightly back in a ponytail revealing a naturally beautiful face, free of makeup, angular with kind hazel eyes that seemed to be seeing right through Robin.

Apologizing for not being able to come sooner, she explained about a big order going out that she had to finish preparing. Frank, her husband, was now packing it up for shipping.

"By the way, my sweet husband sends you his best," Suzanne said with a twinkle in her eye. Robin knew how understanding Suzanne's husband was and what a great partner he turned out to be for her. Robin looked relieved to see her good friend. She needed distraction and a little help.

"I brought over a few meals to put in your refrigerator." Suzanne held up two shopping bags filled with goodies.

"You're awesome, Suzanne. Thank you. Sheesh, I didn't even see or hear you come in."

"Now what can I do for you?"

"Silly me. I stocked up with a case of water but with my arm broken in two places and three broken ribs, I absolutely cannot open the damn bottles. Can you just unscrew all the caps? I was considering chewing through the plastic I was getting so desperate," she chuckled, causing her pain. She steadied her chest movements with her left hand.

Suzanne padded out to the kitchen pantry to take care of the assignment, unpacked the meals into the empty refrigerator, and returned with a treat: a chocolate brownie with walnuts from Robin's much-loved bakery down the street.

"I know it's not healthy, but you need an indulgence." Suzanne laid the unwrapped brownie on the bed in reach of Robin's unbroken arm. Without any hesitation, Robin brought it to her mouth, humming in pleasure.

Suzanne suggested going outdoors for a walk. "Vegetating in bed is not going to encourage healing," she reasoned, and anyhow it was a lovely day. Robin acknowledged that Judy had made the same recommendation, but she hadn't been ready. Today it was worth a try so after wiping the last brownie crumb off her face, she gently threw off the covers and swung her legs gingerly to the side of the bed. Suzanne assisted her into a loose green button-down sundress trying to jostle her as little as possible. She held her good arm for support as they exited slowly down the stairs and into the warm spring day.

The street around the condo was empty as they strolled slowly around the block, taking in the lush wall of ficus trees on one side and neatly manicured gardens on the other graced with palm trees, blossoms of fragrant gardenias, colorful hibiscus and lilies. Robin was moving like an elderly person, but she had to admit she relished being outdoors. She filled her lungs with fresh spring air and enjoyed the heat from the sun radiating into her body. The walk reconnected her to the present moment and the hopeful optimism that she'll be okay…someday.

Suzanne asked about Richard, but Robin seemed ill-inclined to want to talk about him. All she would offer is that he was working in Europe and she didn't know when he'd be back.

Suzanne was compassionate and felt the need to do a little friend stroking, telling Robin what an amazing person she was and how she had so much to give some special person. "For goodness sakes, girlfriend, you need to let someone into that big heart of yours."

Robin was guarded and hesitant to engage in a serious relationship. She feared that even slightly activating her heart muscle would only lead to suffering. She justified keeping layered in protective defenses, too afraid of loss or hurt.

Robin's divorce from John had been hard. She knew he was profoundly wounded when, after 15 years, she wanted a divorce. She could never endure anything like that experience again. How is it possible that one minute you care deeply about a person and the next minute you're arguing and hating one another? How does a relationship morph through such extremes? How can you love so much and then hate so intensely? It did not make any sense. Was there some misplaced neural pathway in her brain that was out of sync? Clearly, she had not realized who John was when they first met.

AWAKENING

Robin and John had fallen madly for each other at warp speed after a happenstance meeting at a local coffee shop. It was close to the cliched "love at first sight." He was attractive with dark, wavy hair and enigmatic light brown eyes that she would lose herself in. He had a strong, muscular build and a protective nature, signaling that he would take good care of his precious Robin. But a year after they got married, John began to show a vastly different personality. He stopped being sweet and attentive and just wanted stuff, a better job, a bigger house, more electronics for his massive entertainment center. His happiness was always deferred to some future point when something monumental would happen to bring him satisfaction. But nothing ever made any difference.

Before they met, John decided that he never wanted to bring children into the world, so he had a vasectomy. Robin had always thought that she would have children, that it was an inevitability. When she and John got serious about being together, he told her that he could always have the surgical knot undone if she genuinely wanted children. But she'd been ambivalent and just accepted the fate of having a menagerie of pets. After they got married, John was more than she could handle. Adding little ones to the scene would have sent her to a sanatorium.

Pure and simple, John was an unhappy guy and no matter what Robin did to make life better, he was always angry and negative. He would get frustrated and upset at even simple things, misplacing a favorite pen, or trash breaking through the bottom of the plastic kitchen bag spewing all over the floor, or a toilet overflowing and wrecking a bathroom throw carpet. Or the laundry getting stuck in the chute that was supposed to deliver dirty clothes from the top-floor bedroom directly to the basement. He'd fly into a rage slamming a drinking glass on a counter, crushing it with his bare hand into knife-like shards that would make his palm bleed. She'd rush him with his hand wrapped in a bloodied kitchen towel to the emergency room for stitches.

One icy winter morning after a storm, John was late for a sales meeting and had left his car in the driveway the night before rather than warmly nestled in the garage. His windshield was covered in a thin layer of slick frozen water blanketed with a pile of snow. He hurriedly scrubbed at the surface with a plastic ice scraper, going so quickly and forcefully that he slipped and smashed his gloved hand so hard into the side view mirror that he broke two of his frosted fingers. He was well-known by all the staff at the ER.

John's anger was mostly self-directed but made Robin feel as if she were somehow the cause of his ill temper. Like the role of many women, she plunged into thinking that she wasn't good enough or didn't love John enough to succeed at marriage. Robin had started to withhold information that might trigger an explosion, like their bank account dwindling too low to pay their mortgage or that she didn't get the magazine assignment that was going to pay big bucks. She walked through her marriage cautiously as if treading on eggshells not wanting to crack through to more of his ire. She isolated herself in her own worries and thoughts for self-preservation.

Robin tried everything. She helped John get a better paying sales job. They bought a bigger, more modern house. They adopted a dog, and then another, added a couple of cats, a very noisy parrot, and tropical fish. They put in a pool, got a sexier sports car. But nothing satisfied him, and they were tumbling into a deep cavern of debt.

After years of trying to be his therapist, mood-booster, and problem solver, she realized that she couldn't be his wife any longer. There was nothing she could do to make him happy. Happiness is an inside job and she no longer felt capable nor blamable. His depression was weighing her down like a cement cape, restricting her interactions with even close friends. When she would leave for a luncheon or an interview, he'd become possessive and suspicious, accusing her of having an affair. She wasn't. She couldn't. She was losing her mind along with her sexuality. She was a blob of flesh and bones that could still write decently enough to keep getting assignments, but she was feeling trapped in a world that was not of her making and in conflict with her being.

The turning point came a year after they had purchased a 5,000-square foot ultra-contemporary house just outside New York City with quarry-tile flooring, skylights and floor-to-ceiling glass windows overlooking a lovely stream on a hilly landscape. The rambling yard was often alive with deer and rabbits that would draw barks and chases from their two golden retrievers. Even though they owned 22 acres, the white-washed architectural masterpiece unfortunately turned out to straddle a boundary line. They had bought the house from a divorce settlement between a wife and her savvy attorney husband and even with surveys and proper closing documents, their dream house was half squatting on the ex-husband's property. It was like their living room and upstairs bedrooms were in one state while the rest of the house resided in another. How was this even possible?

John was ballistic and inconsolable, determined to sue everyone. But there was no easy fix and talk is cheap unless it's to an attorney. There were six attorneys involved representing banks, merged title insurance companies, the ex's lawyers… there was no solution. It was as if they were riding a taxicab with its meter constantly clicking and they could never arrive at a destination. After battling for more than a year, their attorney's fees had climbed to half a million dollars, forcing them to declare bankruptcy and find a new place to live.

John never recovered from the demise of his perceived kingdom, the utter embarrassment of bankruptcy, and the failure, which was a crushing blow to his manhood. He became more abusive and hostile as if everyone in the world was out to get him, to destroy his life. Robin kept trying to cajole him out of his angry state, but she was rattled and overwhelmed. She'd tell him she was with him, by his side. That is, until she wasn't.

She knew she had to get out to save herself, but her exit was devastating. He threatened to start his car in the garage and suck in exhaust fumes. Every day she returned from meetings or researching, with fear of finding him dead in the fancy car they'd been allowed to keep but couldn't afford.

She never told anyone what was going on with her marriage, so when she announced the divorce, her family and friends were shocked. A private person, Robin didn't like gossip and didn't like to share deeply personal experiences that she believed should be confined to just the two people involved. Her marriage was really none of anyone else's business. It was her cross to bear and resolve.

Friends could tell how distraught she was, so they urged her to go to counseling to consider her options or change her mind. After all, 15 years is a long commitment. But she had made up her mind. She was a survivor and leaving John was about being able to live on her terms instead of trying to change the spots on a very depressed dog.

It took a shattering toll. She had been so secretive about the years of marital problems that it undermined her friends' usual unflagging support and, more devastating, it rocked her faith in herself. After divorce papers were signed, she remembered a flood of relief that she no longer had to keep struggling to make John happy. She was free, liberated from the shackle and chains of emotional imprisonment. But then she realized that she no longer knew who she was nor understood what made her happy. No longer half of a couple, she had no identity.

She could have been overjoyed to have a clean canvas on which she could create a whole new life. But she was scared and rudderless, not really knowing in which direction to turn, especially now that she was in her early 40s. She wasn't a kid and couldn't afford the time to dabble in more bad choices.

Oh, how she had yearned for her mother through those years. Her mother would have understood. She would have known exactly what to do. Robin experienced deep grief at the loss of her marriage, added to the incomprehensible loss of her mother and the estrangement of her sister. But in some bottomless recess of her mind, her mother's absence was still tinged with a modicum of hope that maybe, just maybe she would magically reappear and come back into Robin's life. Someday.

CHAPTER SIX

MAY 1994

"We're at The Penis!" blurted Stephanie from the back seat as their silver Citroen pulled in front of the Grand Hôtel Nord-Pinus.

"WOWIE," exclaimed Ruth admiring the facade over the steering wheel.

"Looks like a film set. A place for high society, glamour." Nan was clearly captivated.

"Perfect for the Triple Ts," Stephanie laughed heartily. "Watch out. Here we come."

Dating from the 1920s, the historic boutique hotel oozed charm. Large arched windows accented with gracious shutters and a rounded front entrance and antique sconces harked back to another era. With shadows cast by the leafy plane trees peppering the Place du Forum in the heart of Arles, the renowned hotel could easily conjure up images of Jean Cocteau or Pablo Picasso in black capes strolling into the lobby.

An elegant, grey-haired man graciously welcomed the trio in his impeccable, British-accented English. They marveled at the lobby's display of past glories—old posters of bullfights and memorabilia of the famous artists and writers who frequented the stylish place. They passed leather club chairs and grand archways on the way to their chic, modern and spacious suite complete with a living room and terrace. The Triple Ts ogled the period accents—ornamental wrought iron headboards and a lavish chandelier dangling from the middle of the ceiling.

"It's exquisite," Nan announced breathlessly.

"I never expected this," said Ruth with admiration in her voice. "Especially the deal we got."

"I'll thank my travel agent for you when we get back, "Nan offered.

They settled in quickly. Stephanie headed instantly out onto the terrace and pointed at the yellow café at the corner, drawing her two friends out for a look.

"That's the café made famous by Van Gogh," Nan commented.

"Yes, where he painted the *Café Terrace at Night*. Can't believe we can see it from our room," said Stephanie with delight. "Amazing!"

"Let's do like the natives and go hang out there right now for an aperitif," prompted Ruth. "We'll unpack later."

"I want a pastis," chirped Nan.

"Are we eating?" Stephanie wanted to know.

"It's only 4 o'clock…too early. But what the heck. Let's have a drink and then get our bearings."

"Yeah. Good idea. Put on your walking shoes," advised Ruth.

Installed at an outside table at the café, the three acted at once like sophisticated world travelers as well as little girls getting the best birthday surprise of their lives. Their table looked out on a busy square filled with bustling restaurants alive with activity, albeit a bit quieter in May than the full-blown summer season.

Between jet lag and traveling, the three should've been exhausted but the thrill and exhilaration of being in Provence fueled them with energy. As they sipped pastis, licorice-tasting aperitifs, they scanned their surroundings with wide-eyed satisfaction at being part of this heady experience. They breathed in the warm bustling atmosphere.

The square was surrounded by busy cafés. A bicyclist rode past with baguettes poking out of his basket. A couple held hands as they strolled by with their frisky little dog. They smelled wafting scents of espresso, paella cooking at a nearby brasserie, the staleness of diesel fumes, and hints of perfumes or potpourris. They clinked their glasses and giggled conspiratorially, wondering what their fortnight would bring.

Ruth wanted to see Les Baux and the Camargue and each excursion would likely require a full day on their itinerary. Stephanie wholeheartedly agreed with both options. She remembered in art school seeing *Camargue Secrete*, a book of exquisite black and white photographs that Arles-based photographer Lucien Clergue captured of the fragile and beautiful ecosystem, all taken from a closeup, nose-eye view. Pages were filled with detailed images of the edges of ponds, wind-swept sands, bas reliefs of drought appearing like formidable sculptures in nature, lost in the mists of time and yet traced in this artist's optics.

Stephanie continued, "My photography professor at Parsons claimed he knew Lucien Clergue personally and visited his home here. He said Lucien has a huge bar in his living room that was constructed from the floor of Van Gogh's home. Lucien also founded that big annual photography festival that your neighbor mentioned." She looked at Ruth as she said this.

"Maybe we can drop in on Lucien," Stephanie asked expectantly.

"Oh sure, he'd be open to hosting three American vagabonds," chirped Nan.

"Hey, you never know," Stephanie said, staring at her glass of pastis as if the answer lay within the chalky liquid.

"I'm ready to explore," Nan changed the subject, pulling out her Arles map.

Ruth suggested walking to Les Arenes. "It's supposed to be impressive and not too terribly far from here."

They strolled through the twisting, cobblestoned streets past sun-kissed stone houses, Roman ruins, attractive storefronts, and more cafés. The glow of the Provencal sunlight enhanced the earth-toned terracotta roofs, burnt oranges in the narrow roadways, and pale-yellow buildings laced with green and lavender lilac vines. The scene looked as if it was photo-touched behind polarized lenses, colors so vibrant. The scenery was sharply defined and crystal clear, like looking through the most perfect corrective lenses bringing everything into immaculate focus. No wonder so many artists have been inspired to paint or photograph the deeply saturated, almost unreal tonalities, especially against bluebird skies. Or perhaps the drinks and fatigue were distorting their perceptions.

Ruth was impressed with blooming purple wisteria plants that hung lushly on vines clinging to window ledges overlooking the ancient streets. "Note to self," said Ruth. "I love those purple flowering displays. I wonder if they would thrive where I live. Wouldn't that look beautiful against my pale-yellow house?"

The girls thought it would. "It'd give my home a little French country accent. That would be soooo nice."

"I'd come paint the scene," said Stephanie. "And they're so fragrant."

Ruth got lost in thought for a moment as she envisioned making it happen.

They meandered down Rue du Refuge and noticed a quaint gallery-bookshop called La Natura. A distinctive Frenchman was sweeping debris from beneath iconic French blue shutters, the *volets battants*. He had a touch of gray at his temples and wore khaki slacks and a pressed open-collared blue shirt. He nodded in a friendly gesture to the three ladies just as they paused to peer inside the open door. An elderly bald man was arranging a bookshelf just inside. He looked up at them with an odd smirk, revealing rotted teeth. They glanced beyond to the medieval arches of the interior. Sensing their interest, the *gentihomme* invited them in with a gracious wave of his arm but Nan explained they were on their way to see Les Arenes.

He pointed out the route, adding that they were not far and to please stop back as his gallery was open until 7 o'clock. He introduced himself as Marcel. Nan thanked him as he made sudden, penetrating eye contact with Ruth who had been staring into his warm friendly eyes. Ruth was enamored with him, the store, and the whole moment even though she didn't understand a word of the French exchange that he had with Nan.

As soon as they continued their walk, both Ruth and Stephanie simultaneously asked Nan for translations. Stephanie thought the guy was cute. Ruth was dying to stop there on their walk back to the hotel. "It looks like my kind of place to find amazing books," she justified.

At the next intersection, the marquee attraction of the oval arena appeared and did not disappoint. Modeled after Rome's Coliseum and built a couple of decades after in 90 AD, the amphitheater easily brought to the imagination thoughts of ancient entertainment by gladiators and chariot races. The outside towers were medieval vestiges from the arena's time as a citadel.

Still well-preserved after so many centuries, it was a stunning example of Roman architecture and still part of the city's cultural life. Colorful posters at its entrances announced upcoming bullfights and concerts. "Hard to believe we're seeing more than 2,000 years of history embodied in this," said Nan, gazing up at the immense structure.

Standing in front of one of the massive towers, Ruth stared in reverence. She applauded the designer, the builders. "Can you feel it?," she asked and reflected on the millions of lives that have passed through these high stone arches into the arena itself, some even participating in the ancient games.

"Remarkable to realize that in the States we have old monuments that date back a few hundred years and here…" Stephanie paused to take a breath and Ruth jumped in to finish her thought.

"It's thousands," Ruth gushed. "I wonder about all the people who've come here. I wonder about their stories."

"You mean all the tourists who visit," Nan stated. "I'm sure they come from all over the world to see this place."

"No, the Romans. What was life like for them? Did they choose their lives or was life just thrust upon them? Did they have to conform to society, to the male leadership and their roles? Were the women happy in not having any status other than taking care of their homes and children? Were any of them courageous enough to rebel against the norms of the day?"

"Aren't we being melodramatic!" exclaimed Stephanie, cutting through Ruth's penetrating out-loud thoughts. "Female power," she raised her hand to high-five her girlfriends. "We've come a long way, baby."

Ruth smiled. Her girlfriends should know by now how much she loves a good story and can't help but wonder about life in those days. Just standing on these grounds looking at the Roman masterpiece took her breath away. She'd need to find books about this superpower civilization and the female role.

They continued gawking as they walked admiringly around the colossal building. Stephanie suggested picking another day to take an inside tour. They agreed, deciding for now to explore further down the street.

They strolled past the souvenir shops to the outskirts of town by the Rhone River. In the distance, they noticed a large group of bizarrely and brightly dressed people dancing barefoot on the banks. They were too far away to hear any music, but they could see a group of musicians and behind them a rope hanging between two caravans being used to dry clothes in the open air.

"Gypsies!," shouted Stephanie a little too loudly. "There's some sort of festival they all go to. They come from everywhere."

Ruth stared with rapt attention. Muscular gypsy men wearing black hats danced mostly shirtless with a throng of women in colorful dresses. Little girls with long dark hair threw their bodies wildly in the center wearing pretty flamenco dresses. The spectacle was odd and forbidding. The group looked filthy, strange, and yet seemed so carefree and joyful.

Nan said she'd heard about gypsies, that they just travel from town to town by caravan. She recounted the advice about being careful not to get into any kind of confrontation with them.

"They're volatile," Nan claimed. "They're thieves and break into stores and cars at night to steal stuff. We need to be careful. They can be dangerous."

Nan suggested they get out of there, but Ruth remained fascinated and had a hard time pulling herself away. She felt like a voyeur getting a glimpse of yet another type of lifestyle so foreign from her own. Her friends could almost see her brain working overtime.

"C'mon," urged Stephanie. "Let's stop by that cool gallery."

"Go see Marcel," Nan added with a heavy emphasis on the owner's name as if he were a long-lost friend.

The old man with the bad teeth nodded to the ladies as they entered the attractive shop that was both a bookstore and gallery with a lovely bar offering beers and wines.

"*Ah Mesdames, bienvenues*," cooed Marcel. "*Americaines?*"

"*Oui*," Nan responded.

In almost perfect English, Marcel conveyed his gratefulness that they had come back to visit him. As he said this, he winked at Ruth and her face reddened, not knowing how to react. He offered them a taste of *Chateau Neuf du Pape* that he had just opened. They dipped their heads in acceptance feeling like they were celebrities or royalty being treated so graciously.

He carefully poured a couple of inches of the dark red wine into three large glass goblets and lifted the first offering to Ruth.

"*Merci*, "she said softly using the only word she knew besides *bonjour* and was warmed by his calm eyes and generosity. He had a relaxing demeanor that immediately put everyone at ease, especially Ruth who'd been nervously playing with the silver locket she always wore. Marcel noticed and commented that it was an exceptionally beautiful charm. Ruth blushed, telling him that it was an old piece and incredibly special to her.

He distributed the other two glasses to Nan and Stephanie, acknowledging that it was his pleasure to share this special bottle of wine. He explained that one of his regular clients gifted it to him as a thank you for a special artwork he'd secured. He described how the wine is a bold Grenache-based full-bodied red blend.

They all sipped the wine approvingly. "How is it you speak English so fluently?," Stephanie asked curiously.

Marcel laughed and explained, "We had a young American living with my family until I was ten. Lisa was our *au pair* from Indiana. I was lucky to learn English so young."

Suddenly Ruth interrupted as she got excited to see a photograph of Anaïs Nin hanging in the gallery. Stephanie recognized that it was a portrait done by Man Ray, the American photographer who lived and worked in Paris. Stephanie started to wander around the shop with her elegant glass of wine and Nan joined her as Ruth remained seated at the bar. Ruth was acutely aware of Marcel's physical proximity, the heat of his body standing so close to her and the musty scent of his cologne mixed with the fragrance of the wine. She smiled inwardly.

Marcel acknowledged the accuracy of their observations, adding that he had a show of Man Ray's photographs a few months earlier, but this was the only remaining photograph from that exhibition. He asked Ruth if she liked Anaïs Nin.

"She was a fascinating woman and certainly very progressive for her time," Ruth noted with interest.

Marcel laughed, admitting that was quite an understatement and very diplomatic about such a scandalous person in those days.

"Would you by any chance have her diaries? It would be fun to read them while I'm in France," Ruth asked.

Marcel had several copies, but they were tucked away in a storage facility. He told Ruth that he would be happy to put one aside for her and have it at the shop if she could come back tomorrow. Ruth was overjoyed but instead of tomorrow, asked if she may return the day after. The friends had decided that they would leave in the morning to visit Les Baux and they might be returning too late to stop by.

"No problem," said Marcel, adding that Les Baux de Provence was one of the most beautiful villages in France situated remarkably high on a rocky plateau with brilliant views of Arles. There were also some lovely specialty shops that have particularly good prices on items that are typically made by local artisans.

The Trio got an early start on the dawning of a sun-filled Arlesian morning. After *café au lait* and croissants served in the elegant hotel lounge, they took the short drive to the magical attraction. The village of Les Baux de Provence was indeed as Marcel had described, a dramatic and immense stone village dating back to the Middle Ages. They were so exuberant to be there that the three women practically danced up the cobblestoned streets passing ancient houses, galleries with beautiful Renaissance facades, boutique hotels, cafés and craft shops that were just opening. Shopkeepers carefully placed products on outdoor displays. The ladies' heads were swiveling from side to side with tremendous interest in each shop, but they had agreed to start at the farthest lookout point.

As they approached the rocky embankment, the wind began to whip into a frenzy and Stephanie held tight to her navy beret. Ruth put her hand on the front of her ankle-length flowing skirt to keep it from inverting embarrassingly. Nan, in shorts and a collared shirt, tried to keep her hair from flogging her face and with a quick upward sweep she secured it into a messy bun at the top of her head with a clip.

As the landscape revealed itself, they were spellbound by the vista. The Alpilles Mountain range stood as a majestic background covered in scrubland, pine, and oak forests. Patches of verdant plains and fields of olive trees stretched as far as the eye could see, dotted by private stone residences with clay-tiled roofs in every direction. The unique radiance of the south-of-France sun and crisp air created a mesmerizing panorama against the cobalt heavens.

"What a vantage point," exclaimed Stephanie. "I'd like to put my easel right here." She gestured to a small grassy area nearby.

"Makes sense how the area was used as a fortress," Ruth commented. "You'd certainly be aware of anyone approaching."

"For sure," said Nan as a whopping gust thrust her hair back across her face. She struggled to get it under control. "I love this view, but I've got to get out of the windstorm."

They wandered away from the edge and were immediately drawn into Flora Atelier, an enticing little shop filled with unusual and decorative floral items. Tiny tubes and squares contained lovely natural flowers, trays with sweet multicolored wisps, glass boxes with lively arrangements. The artist-owner explained that all the flowers were native to the area. Stephanie could not resist buying a gorgeous paper-wrapped arrangement of assorted dried blossoms in hues of blues, purples and yellows. She decided they must add the beautiful visual display to their hotel room. Nan and Ruth nodded enthusiastically.

They decided to visit the atelier next door crammed with stunning Provencal fabrics of florals and fruits in pastels, yellows, oranges, and greens. Nan instantly wanted the country table linens for summer entertaining. Ruth fell in love with a square azure cotton scarf bedecked with olives and olive branches. As soon as she paid for her treasure, she folded it into a triangle and wrapped it around her neck. It was the perfect accent to her long monochromatic navy skirt and cap-sleeved ecru blouse. She was instantly transformed into a *mademoiselle*.

"*Tres charmante*," said the shop owner, seeing Ruth's new appearance.

"That scarf makes the outfit," noted Stephanie. "Good colors for you. But seeing those olives makes me hungry."

They laughed and Nan suggested their next stop be one of the *creperies*. Seated outside at La Celtie de Provence, they could happily watch the pedestrians on the street. They relished their feathery thin pancakes—a staple of France. Stephanie had ham and Gruyere cheese. Nan's were filled with scrambled eggs and ratatouille, topped with chevre. Ruth feasted on a crispy galette with chicken, lightly cooked apple, caramelized onions and topped with foie gras. They complemented their savory lunch with a pitcher of house cider.

"And for dessert…" Stephanie announced.

"You go, girl," retorted Nan. "I'm stuffed."

"But they're so light," sassed Stephanie, ordering a Gâteau Feuilleté. Her eyes grew wide when the plate arrived stacked a foot high with crepes on top of each other, layered with pastry cream and topped with caramelized sugar.

"A taste, please?" Ruth reached over and took a small piece. "Sweet!," she exclaimed. "It's going right to my hips."

"Oh yeah, like you have anything to worry about, you skinny minnie," chided Stephanie.

"Now, now children!," Nan was clearly amused. "Behave."

Instead of requesting the check by asking for *l'addition*, Nan cleverly requested *la douleureuse*, meaning the bad news, to which she got a completely empty expression from the arrogant garcon.

Back on the street, Ruth talked about wanting to find something nice to bring back for Jean and Robin. Just as she was discussing her desires, the next shop offered more options. All three gawked over the potpourri exquisitely made from local petals, artisan soaps in all shapes and sizes with amazing fragrances, essential oil hand creams, and body oils. They felt like they had landed in nirvana, overcome by the mixture of competing aromas.

"I think I'm getting lightheaded," Ruth joked as she picked out several items to purchase.

"I'd like one of each," said Stephanie waving her hand across the entire store as if she were a wizard creating magic with her wand.

Nan was animated over the do-it-yourself sachets. She scooped petals of lavender into one, roses into another, bitter orange into a third, like a kid in a candy store.

"Look at those," Ruth chirped, pointing to a display of small ceramic textured white objects.

Stephanie swooped in, "Ah, La Boule de Provence is a special design handcrafted by artisans. Beautiful, isn't it?" She picked one up to demonstrate. "In the heart of the ball is a fragrance that comes through these little holes and carries into the air of a room."

Ruth wanted to know how Stephanie knew so much about these beautiful but expensive items. Stephanie just laughed, admitting she'd just read their story on the wall poster. "Over there," she pointed.

"Smarty pants," giggled Ruth.

They shopped their way through more specialty boutiques. One was wall to wall candies called *calissons*. Another was entirely devoted to olive oils, replete with tastings. Another featured dry biscuits to dunk in teas, with a complement of *confiture*–jams in peach, strawberry, apricot, and cherry flavors. The girls were tickled and entertained by their discoveries, as if no one else in the world knew of these unique places although millions visited annually. They stopped at another lookout point for a final view and then headed back to Arles, delighted with all their shopping bags.

They readied for the evening. Ruth donned a light blue sundress with her new statement scarf tied loosely at her neck. She admired herself in the bathroom mirror telling herself she was looking quite chic.

She emerged to find Nan and Stephanie already dressed and waiting for her. "It's about time, "charged Stephanie impatiently.

She and Nan were both stylishly clothed in black slacks and white blouses.

"Gee, I didn't get the message about tonight's uniform," Ruth said, noticing their outfits.

"An accident…and not exactly the same," said Nan, who topped the look with an orange hued light sweater worn preppy-style, its empty sleeves tied in front.

Stephanie wrapped herself in a long, gauzy, rainbow-colored cape. "Yeah, we have our differences." She smirked.

Ruth laughed. "Yep, in many ways!," she quipped, not missing a beat.

"You look great," Nan said, complimenting Ruth.

"Thanks. I'm feeling much better."

When they first returned from Les Baux in late afternoon, there was a message waiting from Ruth's husband, Teddy, indicating that it was urgent he speak with her. She immediately called him and got the news about several accounting issues at the business regarding files that Ruth had worked on. He complained that errors she'd made were creating serious and expensive penalties. The conversation turned into a boisterous argument.

When Ruth hung up, she was clearly shaken. Nan consoled her as Ruth confessed she felt that Teddy's call was a ploy to make her feel guilty about being so far away for so long. She doubted she'd made such critical errors. She was always so careful in the work she did for the business. Teddy was angry and made no bones about blaming Ruth. In fact, lately he'd been blaming Ruth for a lot of things that weren't going quite right in their lives. Ruth felt the weight of the accusations but more importantly she was upset by their months-long emotional distance.

"If I didn't know better, I'd think he was having an affair." Ruth whispered so low that Nan had trouble hearing her. She spoke in a way that if she said it quietly enough, none of it would be true.

Her face was flushed with emotion and she mindlessly held her silver locket as if it held the answers.

Nan counseled that she needed to trust her instincts and face her fears. Bottling these anxieties was worse than dealing with whatever the reality happens to be. But right now, she needed to give herself permission to enjoy her vacation. She could deal with everything when she returned home. She'd have a renewed outlook and a better sense of what she wanted.

"Does that make sense?," Nan asked, to which Ruth just dropped her head in resigned acknowledgment.

"It'll all be fine," Ruth said. "Let's get on with our evening."

In a subdued mood, the Triple Ts headed out to the luxurious L'hôtel Jules César. Sitting on the restaurant's terrace, they clinked their flutes of *Champagne Framboise* as they gazed out into the brilliance of the setting sun.

Nan suggested that they hold on to the memory of this moment. She guided them to notice the colors of the sun, the sky, their surroundings, the smells, tastes, the sounds of cars shifting gears as they cruised along the Boulevard des Lices in front of them.

Ruth closed her eyes tightly and took a deep breath in, releasing it with a sigh. Her imagination was spinning.

Both Nan and Stephanie started laughing loudly at how seriously focused Ruth looked. Her eyes fluttered open. She giggled and toasted her glass in the air. "Definitely doing better," she asserted to both sets of watchful and concerned eyes.

As they finished ordering from the menu of the Michelin five-star *Lou Marquès*, the hotel's restaurant, they turned their attention to the next day's activities. They discovered from signs posted in the hotel lobby that the boulevard they were on was the site of a popular market in the mornings so they decided that would be their first order of business.

Ruth reminded them that she wanted to pick up the Anaïs Nin diary. "That's right," teased Stephanie. "You have a date with Marcel." Ruth blushed but said nothing.

The haute cuisine meal was exquisite and beautifully presented in the classy and stylish terrace setting. They shared an appetizer of sautéed escargots. Stephanie inhaled her grilled steak entree with artichoke risotto. Ruth remarked that the golden sea bream was done to perfection accompanied with rich-tasting mashed potatoes and offered tastes around the table. Nan enjoyed the turbot with crisp vegetables. They shared crepe soufflé for dessert.

After dinner, the three women were grateful to have a nice walk back to their hotel after their gourmet dinner. "If that were my last supper, I'd die a happy woman," Ruth kidded, patting her full tummy.

They were tired after the long day of sightseeing, shopping, and eating. Ruth was especially spent from her added burden of the disturbing phone encounter with Teddy. They all slept very soundly.

Le Marché d'Arles turned out to be even bigger and more amazing than they anticipated. They arrived before the 8 a.m. official opening and watched with amusement as the vendors aggressively jockeyed for positions. The street was quickly abuzz with hawking merchants, local residents, immigrants, and tourists. Considering all the olive groves they had seen scattered across the terrain from the heights of Les Baux, it was no surprise to see many stands displaying dozens of varieties of olives, and locally-sourced olive oils packaged in bottles and tins.

A feast for the senses, the market's stalls spanned miles, overflowing with vegetables, gigantic wheels of cheese, breads of all shapes and forms, fresh fish, rotisserie chickens, specialties from the eastern Mediterranean, then rows of household goods from towels to tablecloths to dresses, purses and other accessories. It was a colorful combination of a farmers' market and a flea market. The atmosphere was lively and the smells were rich and heady.

Ruth wore dark brown slacks and a pale blue tunic adorned with her new statement scarf. She wore oversized earrings and a chunky leather belt to cinch the sheer fabric of her long shirt. She had on comfortable walking flats and was clearly in a renewed state of mind to seize the day. The weather was unseasonably warm so both Nan and Stephanie were dressed in shorts. Nan's well-tailored collared shirt was topped with her ever-popular cardigan. Stephanie wore an oversized tee shirt and was draped in her colorful, lightweight cape.

"We should've had breakfast here," Stephanie said, eyeing all the enticing-looking rings of warm breads. Nan wasn't paying any attention as she was too absorbed in buying a bag of *herbes de Provence,* a mixture of rosemary, savory basil, thyme, and marjoram. She explained that she was planning to use it to add a dash of flavor to pork chops or chicken back home.

Ruth approached a fruit seller to get a single apple for a morning snack. Using her hands to gesture as to what she wanted, the elderly Algerian who ran the shop simply gave her the apple of her choice, for free! "Wow," reacted Stephanie. "It must be your magic scarf." "No doubt!" Ruth retorted.

They ambled for hours through the sights and sounds, communicating as best they could with farmers and locals, learning much and appreciating the region's people and delicacies. They were delighted at every turn and at ease in the friendly surroundings.

Nan roamed onward and became engaged in the rows of antiques sellers. Ruth found herself getting bored, so she suggested that she run the errand to pick up her book and meet the girls back at Place du Forum for lunch in an hour. "Oh right, you're seeing Marcel," Stephanie taunted.

Ruth reddened. "I'm just picking up the book."

"Go, have fun," Nan waved her hand as if dismissing Ruth as she got more and more immersed in the vintage items spread out in front of her. "Okay, see you back at the Forum!" Ruth called as she strolled away, gleefully re-energized to be on a mission to get her Anaïs Nin diaries.

Stephanie watched her get swallowed up in the crowds and disappear.

An hour later, Nan and Stephanie were back at the café near their hotel. They ordered two glasses of rosé wine and paté to share while they waited for Ruth. A storm suddenly rolled in, the skies darkened, and the temperatures dropped considerably. They decided to move indoors, grabbing their glasses, just as large droplets of rain began to pelt at them. They hurried inside.

"That was rather rude of the weather," Nan remarked. "I wonder where Ruth has gotten to."

"Probably just got lost. It is hard to navigate these circuitous roads," said Stephanie.

But two hours later, with the streets still slick from the heavy rainstorm that had now subsided, they decided to find their way to Marcel's bookstore to check on Ruth.

"*Ah mesdames,*" Marcel greeted them warmly. "What can I do for you today?"

Nan asked if Ruth had come by to pick up the book she ordered when suddenly the answer was obvious. Nan spotted Ruth's blue and yellow scarf curled up on the end of the bar. Marcel followed her eyes. "Yes, yes. We had a nice visit. She was happy to have the book and then the rains came just as she was leaving. She got soaked and came back in to dry off." He handed Ruth's scarf to Nan. "She left this."

"So, when did she leave and where did she go?," asked Nan. She couldn't tell if Marcel looked puzzled or guilty, but a strange look came over him.

"I don't know," he said in a perturbed tone. "She wasn't sure of the way back so Pierre, my assistant, walked her in the right direction. "When was that?," asked Stephanie.

"I'm not sure. I had a few clients here so maybe an hour ago."

Nan reasoned that she must be back at the hotel by now and she and Stephanie thanked Marcel and left.

When they entered their spacious room at the hotel, it was empty. No Ruth and no sign that she had been there. Stephanie plopped down on one of the beds. "What should we do?"

"I'm not sure," said Nan, quietly trying to figure out a solution, an explanation. Maybe she got hungry and stopped for a snack. Maybe she went shopping in those cute stores on the streets near Marcel's store.

"Maybe something happened," Stephanie finally exclaimed, acknowledging the elephant in the room, her voice charged with concern.

Determined that there had to be a plausible explanation, Nan headed to the front desk with Stephanie on her heels. The nice gray-haired gentleman who had greeted them on their first day was there. Nan questioned him as to whether he had seen Ruth recently. He was deeply sorry, but he had not seen her at all today. Not wasting any time, Nan headed outdoors and back to the café where she and Stephanie had been waiting earlier for Ruth to join them. She found their waiter and asked if he had seen their dark-haired petite friend. He had not. Stephanie turned to look at Nan. They were both getting more worried with each passing moment.

"Where the hell is she?," screamed Stephanie. They returned to the Hôtel Nord Pinus. "This cannot be happening," Nan declared.

"Maybe she ran away with the gypsies," said Stephanie.

"This is no time to joke."

"I'm not kidding. You saw the way she watched them…and with trouble on the home front…"

"Oh, stop being ridiculous. Let's figure this out," barked Nan.

Four more frantic hours passed, and Ruth had still not returned to the hotel. Her clothes were on the bed and hanging in their shared closet. Her toiletries stood in a line, untouched in the bathroom. Gifts she'd bought at Les Baux for Jean and Robin were on a night table. Nan ran Ruth's scarf through her fingers trying to make some sense of what was happening.

Nan went back to the front desk and inquired about procedures for reporting a missing person. It was now eight hours since Stephanie watched Ruth dissolve into the crowds of the market.

By midnight, Nan and Stephanie were consumed in panic. They contacted the local police who advised getting in touch with the U.S. Consulate in Marseille. But it was now after hours so they would need to dial the after-hours number of the U.S. Embassy in Paris.

The officious deep-voiced consular officer who answered the call introduced himself as Anthony Barbet. He asked for full identification of both Nan and Stephanie, their passport numbers, contact information, where they were staying, and their relationship to the missing person. He then requested all of Ruth's identifications, plus when and where Ruth Stevens had last been seen. They were asked to supply a photograph of her.

"Do you have contact names of anyone who might know the person's whereabouts?," he asked routinely. Nan told them about Marcel and Pierre.

Ruth was gone. No one had seen her since Pierre walked her into the street and pointed her in the right direction. No one could imagine what had happened. Ruth had evaporated into thin air.

CHAPTER SEVEN

*T*hree months had passed since Robin's accident. She had some ongoing stiffness and aches from her broken bones and concussion but for the most part she was doing well, at least physically.

She tentatively resumed her life. She re-entered her everyday world of writing assignments, dinners with friends, and enjoying beach walks or outings to the area's unique nature preserves.

Richard was still gallivanting around Europe on his film shoots. She enjoyed getting his periodic newsy emails. He'd been to Lisbon, London, back to Lisbon and now was in Venice. Between jobs, he'd been able to spend long weekends in Paris with his brother-in-law and nephew, Philippe, in their cramped apartment on Rue Raymond Losserand in the 15th arrondissement. Richard complained that the place was right next to a bakery which was always tempting him with enticing smells of fresh-baked pastries, but he had to keep his svelte physique for the cameras.

Only three blocks away was *Parc Georges-Brassens*, built on the site of a former fish and horse market. Some of the old structures still stood but the main feature was a large pond, bordered by lawns and groves of trees. Richard would take Philippe to float a toy boat or to scramble up the rock wall, a jumble of artificial stones for children to climb. The boy had natural athleticism. His dark wavy hair would fly wildly during the ascent. When he reached the top, he'd turn his green eyes to check if Richard were watching, which he always was.

He'd blink his long lashes and smile pridefully. Richard would mock clapping and smile back.

After the *Parc*, Richard and Philippe would walk to the cozy neighborhood bistro *Café Arthur et Juliette* with its unpretentious vibe, and sweetly named after the owner's two children. Philippe's father worked long, odd hours managing a restaurant on the Right Bank, so he had no objection to Richard occupying his son as much as he wanted. Uncle and nephew grabbed a seat on the terrace where they could see the bulls guarding their *Parc* as they lunched together.

Sometimes they'd take the Metro to the 18th arrondissement and spend the day around Montmartre, known for its artistic history. Its large hill was topped off like whipped cream with the white-domed Basilica of the *Sacré-Cœur*. It was fun to watch local artists at work in the square and the gawking tourists milling around. Afterwards, they'd stop at the restaurant where Philippe's dad worked.

Keep those emails coming, Robin would write back in response to Richard's emails about his adventures with Philippe. Sounds like quality time with your nephew. He's a lucky boy.

She missed Richard but never admitted it in any of her responses. She was too afraid of attachment and it was safer not to commit. She couldn't get hurt that way, or so she thought.

A serious relationship required too many compromises, she rationalized. But today she was feeling so very alone, and old. Right now, even a compromised relationship seemed mildly attractive just so she didn't have to feel so empty. Richard was not only drop-dead handsome, but he was kind and had diverse interests that made conversations engaging. New thoughts pummeled her brain. But he is a lot younger and he travels so much. And has a narcissistic streak although it comes with the work he does. Her mind was whizzing through scenarios.

Thankfully, Judy saved the day in her knowing way. She interrupted Robin's lonely wallowing with a phone call to suggest a weekend getaway for much-needed renewal at the ashram where they first met a decade ago.

"What an awesome idea." Robin didn't hesitate a millisecond as she was more than ready for a serene yet empowering time, especially with her dearest friend Judy. It was Thursday and they'd leave around noon on Friday.

An empty evening stretched before Robin. It wouldn't take long to pack for the weekend, and she didn't feel like working. What should I do? She needed to get out, away from her head to stop all the thoughts of lonesomeness. Turbulent energies clawed at her insides. She felt an urgent frenzy to do something to change this mental battle and ban the sickening feelings she had in her gut.

She hated when she felt like this, like she didn't belong in the world. Maybe her ex-husband's malaise had caught up with her. Or maybe she was just a worthless mess in her own right. She knew tomorrow would be better with the escape to the ashram. But what now? Beach. Sunset. Nature was her elixir. She could already imagine the silky sand under her bare feet. No two beach experiences were ever the same. Even though she felt unmotivated and lazy, she would push herself to go and would see what tonight would bring.

Deciding she needed people, she rode her bicycle over to Edgewater, a beach front hotel with a bar that spilled out onto the sand. A guitarist was playing his heart out, strumming Jimmy Buffet-style songs and singing badly into a microphone. Looking at the scene from a distance with her feet buried in the smooth white sand, Robin watched locals mingling with hotel guests, laughter mixing with loud conversations. Tropical drinks decorated with tiny umbrellas were in the hands of a few people seated at the bar, others had wine glasses and were gesturing wildly to one another. A cluster of kids chased Frisbees on the adjacent great lawn. Turning towards the Gulf, Robin observed couples holding hands as they strolled the water's edge. Runners jogged. Small groups of women were on an evening stroll but mostly not moving as they gabbed to one another.

"Look," shrieked a young boy excitedly pointing to two dolphins frolicking right in front of him. Tourists were perched awkwardly trying to take selfies with the dolphin backdrop. The sunset was beginning to glow fluorescent yellows and oranges as bathers splashed in the waters.

Robin had had enough of the crowds and walked a few blocks to a quieter stretch. She plopped down in the thicker sand by the beach entrance, near a bunch of large round-leaved sea grapes and tall, elegant sea oats. She took a full breath. The Gulf, calm as a lake, was painted fire red as the sun moved closer to the horizon line, clouds becoming flamboyant pink. Pelicans flew in groups across the changing sky. A few white ibis with long, down-curved orange bills probed for food in the hard sand at the water's edge. A bind of sandpipers hopped daintily near the ebbing and flowing tide. Gentle ripples lapped the shore. The golden orange orb seemed like a teardrop as it touched the surface of the Gulf, slipping lower and lower. A flood of gratitude descended over Robin unexpectedly. She was all alone and yet felt a joy, a connection to something greater. She had rekindled a thankfulness that she was living in this warm, beautiful place. She'd be okay.

~

With a shared spontaneity, Judy and Robin drove for hours until they at last passed through the distinctive red brick walled frontage and wrought iron gates leading to a yogi's paradise. The hushed stillness was pervasive throughout the meandering wide fields nestled along the shoreline of a magnificent lake. The parking area bordered a thriving organic garden which the chef relied on to create delectable vegan meals. As they unfolded from the cramped car, they were filled with a feeling of familiarity about leaving the world out there. Here they were safe, removed from worries and fears. They could be immersed in the energies of this special secluded environment with the spiritual overtones of a deep yogic heritage. They could reignite their heart center and align mind and body. They could quiet their minds and go deep within to experience that integrated place where miracles happen. They had registered for the meditation weekend.

No sooner had they dropped off their bags in their small room when they found themselves in the meditation room, barefoot, sitting on yoga mats cross-legged, backs straight, eyes closed. A senior instructor was guiding the class into continuous streams of Aum. Auuuuummmmmmm. Auuuuuummmmm, Aummmmmmm. All the student's voices collided into one mega reverberation.

Robin felt the vibrational impact of the sounds in the form of sensations in her body bringing her a sense of joy. Now it was time to focus on the third eye in the middle of the forehead and drop into silence.

Suddenly Robin was engulfed by a wave of deep sadness and a hollowness in the pit of her stomach. It gripped her so fast and so furiously that it forced her to bolt for the exit door. She landed on a bench outside gulping the cool air and suddenly sobbing uncontrollably.

What is going on? She tried to regain control. What the hell has come over me? And then she remembered. Today was the anniversary of the day her life was turned on its head. No, not from the motorcycle accident which did a good job in forcing her to re-examine her life's choices. But it was more than half her lifetime ago. It was exactly 25 years ago today when her mother had gone missing in the South of France and Robin's world had been forever changed.

She had no ability to stop the rushing waterfall of tears. It was like she was hypnotized. Her rational mind observed her throbbing body heaving uncontrollably. Sounds came from deep within, strange half screams, half choking gasps. She was almost possessed by the young grieving NYU coed of the past, as if that person were inhabiting her body, shaking her to the core and all she could do was let it happen and watch.

It was hard to know how much time had passed before Robin had the strength to stand. Weak and wobbly, she shuffled slowly over the grassy meadow to the narrow wooden dock that extended out into the blue waters of the lake. She made it halfway to the end and collapsed onto the rough, bare dark planks. The surface felt warm from the sun beating on it all day. Robin could feel the heat penetrating her skin and it helped her relax. She gazed at the beauty spread out before her and dropped her face into her palms. With her fingertips, she gently massaged her eyes, moving to her brows, circling her temples, cheekbones and along her nose. The sensations were soothing. She was coming back to the present, releasing the dark heaviness. She continued stroking her face, running her fingers all along her jawbone, her ears. Then she buried her face fully in her hands, took a deep, cleansing breath and simply announced to herself *I'm okay*.

As if echoing her thoughts, a voice bellowed, "You okay?" Robin immediately recognized Judy's gravelly tone without turning around to look. Judy walked briskly out to where Robin was seated and ran her hand across Robin's shoulders in a comforting gesture. "I figured I'd find you here. Do you want to talk?"

Robin just wanted to return to the meditation room and start again. Judy told her that dinner was about to be served. Perhaps they should eat and afterwards take a nice country walk. Robin nodded in agreement.

After dinner, instead of walking with Judy, Robin wandered down to the edge of the lake where she knew she could find the best phone reception. Her hands shaking, she pulled up the contact number for Nan Peters and pushed the little green phone symbol. The phone immediately dialed and Nan, her mom's closest childhood friend who was the key person to deal with all the missing person inquiries on that fateful day, was on the other end of the phone. Robin tried to speak in response to her calm "Hello," but the words got stuck in her throat.

Finally, on the third repetition of hello, Robin haltingly choked out, "Nan, this, this… is… Robin, Ruth's daughter."

Nan and Robin had stayed in touch over the years. To Robin, Nan was like an aunt, a person she'd known her entire life, someone she always knew was part of her family. They usually spoke around the holidays to wish each other well but rarely saw one another.

Once, about a dozen years ago when Robin was still living in Greenwich Village, Nan had met her for lunch at Paesano's, a classic Italian restaurant in a rustic setting on Mulberry Street in Little Italy. The lobster ravioli was Robin's favorite. Nan had enjoyed the chicken Francaise and raved about the wood-beamed ceilings and the coziness of the place.

Robin liked Nan but spending time with her was bittersweet. She enjoyed the familiar relationship and Nan's caring warmth, but Nan became a painful reminder of what Robin had lost. Still, Robin appreciated Nan's expertise as a psychotherapist and her generosity in being there for her when she needed a shoulder or advice. Nan reiterated the offer to use her as a sounding board or for help at any time she needed a "motherly" point of view. "Your mom would have wanted me to serve you in any way I could. I owe it to her…and to you," Nan had said as she'd sipped her Pellegrino and pushed back her own waves of emotions. On several occasions since, Robin had reached out and was always rewarded with authentic kindness and valuable strategies.

In typical Nan style, her voice was full of openness and comfort. In between muffled sobs, Robin explained that she'd just had a meltdown on this auspicious anniversary day. During more than two decades of her mother being classified as a missing person, Robin had stuffed down her feelings. She still had this gaping cavern in the center of her heart that was black and hollow. Nan steadily explained that her feelings were totally understandable for someone who had endured this type of trauma. "You've never had closure for the loss of your mother," Nan said delicately. "You'll never resolve that emptiness if you don't face it."

"How?" Robin asked. Nan offered a few simple suggestions, but nothing resonated until a thought about retracing Ruth's steps bubbled to the surface. "Perhaps seeing and experiencing the places Ruth had been would allow you to reconnect and release the past in the present. You've never been able to have a funeral or officially say goodbye to your mom. Perhaps being in the spirit of that place would allow you to have something real to let go of and a different kind of understanding. I doubt you'll get any concrete answers to what happened but perhaps you'll intuitively connect to your mother. Energy never dies. I know she's still there."

Robin seized the idea and asked Nan if she would go with her. At first, Nan was silent. Reliving that experience was something she'd done millions of times, in dreams, in daily thoughts, in moments when she'd seen fabrics reminding her of Ruth's magical scarf. She searched her soul in that millisecond of hesitation and decided that she could also benefit from closure. "To be perfectly frank," she started, "It's not something I really want to do but I can see now that I have to. So yes."

Nan quietly suggested taking a week the following month and wondered what Robin thought of inviting the other witness to that event, her mom's other childhood friend Stephanie. In fact, Nan was well aware of the powerful timing of today and had left a voice message for Stephanie that afternoon. She was awaiting a return call and would like to extend an invitation if Robin were okay with that. Nan wasn't sure Stephanie would even accept as she, too, had wrestled with that fateful day of upheaval and desperation being in a foreign country and dealing with the realities of your close friend vanishing into thin air. How can anyone reconcile such a horror? Robin felt reassured about the plans to visit Arles with Nan and, if willing, Stephanie.

"I have one more thought," Nan sounded tentative, becoming silent for several beats.

"What is it?" Robin sounded impatient yet curious.

"How do you feel about inviting your sister?"

Robin giggled nervously avoiding a knee-jerk answer. She calculated her response.

"You can ask…" Robin's voice was filled with a doubt that hung in the air.

"Maybe she, too, could benefit," Nan said awkwardly.

"Maybe… I guess…" Robin resented Nan even asking and knew it would be unpleasant to have Jean on this expedition into the past. Jean would dampen everyone's spirits with her negativity. They hadn't spoken in a few years and she hated Robin. Robin hoped she wouldn't have to deal with Jean through what she was anticipating being a difficult, emotionally wrenching trip. She'd be a Debbie Downer to drag along.

"Ask her," she squeaked out at last, trying to sound positive.

Robin tossed the resolution to fate: what would be would be. It was out of her control. Satisfied that she had a logical plan, Robin went in search of Judy who she found lounging in their shared bedroom in the ashram's main house. The room was a hodge-podge of furnishings with two twin beds, but its best feature was the view of the sliver of lake from one window.

Judy had been quietly reading on a worn wooden rocker next to a standing lamp that looked like it came from a barn sale and generated a pitiful amount of dim light. Robin barreled through the door causing Judy to quickly glance up and peer over the top of her tablet. Judy looked deeply into Robin's eyes. "You're different."

Robin told her about the phone call with Nan and the plans to revisit the place where her mother had disappeared. Judy knew this time had been long coming, inevitable and totally necessary for Robin's future. Robin had closed off a large part of her heart and her ability to experience love. For a quarter century, Robin had equated love with loss and tragedy. Fear kept her from truly feeling the deep joys of love, the essence of all, of harmony and well-being. And denying those emotions trapped sadness, blame and negativity within her body.

Every cell was tainted with a low vibrational frequency that would eventually cause the body to malfunction and dis-ease to emerge. Without being able to release the deep ugliness that haunted every fiber of her being, affecting her mentally, emotionally and physically, Robin was destined to suffer and would never realize her potential. Judy applauded Robin's courage to step up and was awed that Nan was willing to go back and re-create that time.

"You're so lucky that your mom had such an amazing friend in Nan," Judy chirped.

Instantly Robin responded, "Like us." She smiled.

Judy sprang out of the chair, wrapping her arms tightly around Robin and hugging her so hard that Robin suddenly found the moment funny as she broke out laughing. Judy joined the cathartic release.

"Wait, I have something." Judy spun around to her suitcase perched at the foot of the bed and unzipped a special compartment filled with small brown vials. She put on a pair of cheaters camouflaging her blue eyes. She wore a loose-fitting white short-sleeved blouse with a tiny eyelet ruffle around the collar, over white yoga pants. Her long blond hair was bunched haphazardly on the top of her head. She carefully studied her stash looking like a mad scientist and selected two small bottles along with a container of jojoba oil.

'Open your hands." She showed Robin how to cup them so that both palms were open to the sky. She poured the golden jojoba liquid until it pooled in one palm. Then she added two drops of therapeutic grade clary sage and two drops of bergamot.

"Now rub your hands together blending all the oils. Okay, bring your palms to your face and inhale deeply."

"Ummmmmmm, nice," exclaimed Robin.

"Now rub the mixture onto your neck, back of your neck, chest and then all over your hands."

"Sooooo very calming."

"Good. It's doing what it's supposed to do. This brew quiets emotions."

Judy appreciated the opportunity to share her aromatherapy training with her close friend who was clearly in need. It was so rewarding to be able to impact someone's well-being naturally without the use of pharmaceuticals, which used to be part of her treatment protocols when she practiced nursing. What used to be regarded as esoteric or "woo-woo" had gone mainstream. Even Mayo Clinic had reported on how concentrated essential oils activate smell receptors that send messages through the nervous system to the brain's limbic system where emotions are controlled. Some oils impact the hypothalamus, releasing feel-good brain chemicals. What you put on your skin accesses the bloodstream in less than 30 seconds. Judy had taken this practice seriously and found oils that help reduce pain, panic attacks, anxiety, stress, grief, sadness, and depression, all infinitely preferable to fabricated chemicals that the pharmacies peddle.

"Now about that walk," said Robin, feeling revived as if no time had elapsed since their original discussion. "Is it too late?" "Not at all," said Judy.

With a flashlight at the ready, they linked arms and sauntered out into the cool night air and along the dirt path. They said nothing and just relished the delicious togetherness and moment of being.

The next day, Nan called to confirm that Stephanie would join them in the South of France and that her travel agent would establish the itinerary.

Jean had declined. Robin wanted to know more about Jean's decision but refrained from asking as whatever she said would only be an aggravation. Better to be quiet. They decided on specific dates and agreed to make arrangements the following week.

On the drive back to Naples with Judy at the wheel, Robin made an overseas call to Richard to let him know she would be traveling to France in three weeks. She asked if he would have time to see her before she embarked on her journey into the dark past in Arles.

Richard was ecstatic that Robin would be in Europe but around that time he was going to be in London. Robin surged with disappointment until Richard suggested she spend a few days with him in London and then fly to Marseille.

Plans were seamlessly dropping into place and Robin felt both elated and frightened by thoughts of the trip, being with Richard after such a long separation and, most importantly, delving into areas about her mother's disappearance that maybe should be left buried in the past.

Reading her thoughts, Judy put her mind at ease. "You're doing all the right things. It will all work out one way or another."

Robin wasn't exactly sure what Judy meant by "one way or another" but she'd faced enough of her fears for the moment and wasn't going to open another Pandora's box just yet.

The weeks of preparation flew past in a whirlwind of activity. Nan had worked out the most minute details. She even confirmed that Marcel still owned his gallery-bookstore and prepared him for their visit. Finally, Suzanne was driving Robin to Miami for the flight to Heathrow where Richard would be waiting. The timing had worked out well as Suzanne had to meet an incoming shipment of fabrics coming through international customs. The friends talked about Robin's upcoming escapades during the two hour drive from Naples across Alligator Alley to Miami. As they chatted, Robin could feel a tingling sensation rising in her spine with crazy anticipation.

CHAPTER EIGHT

EARLY JUNE 2019

*R*ichard looked fine in blue jeans, tee shirt and close-fitting brown leather jacket. His blue eyes sparkled as he whisked Robin off her feet with a hug and a sloppy kiss at the airport and then pushed back his dark wavy curls that had fallen into his eyes. Prepared for any kind of London weather, Robin wore a long, fitted trench coat over yoga pants topped with a slim tunic. Being a motorcyclist, Robin had learned to travel very economically when it came to luggage. She had only a carry-on bag, so they were on the damp London streets in no time.

Richard was doing a shoot for a major cosmetics company and they had housed him in a lovely flat within bell-ringing distance of Big Ben in the heart of Westminster. Robin was impressed and grateful to have such an exquisite, albeit small apartment, in which to hang out with Richard for a couple of days.

Richard seemed enthralled to see Robin and had made plans for their first day if Robin was up for jumping into the swing of things. As he shared plans, Robin rubbed her hand across the scruff on his face which looked good with his rugged features and structured jawline.

"For the shoot?" He nodded affirmatively.

By day, he suggested an orientation of London with a walk along the River Thames footpath between London Bridge and Greenwich district, passing landmarks like the Tower of London and stylish

Canary Wharf. Robin approved enthusiastically.

For the evening, Richard intended to take Robin to the Night Market in Perks Field near Kensington Gardens. As part of London Food Month, this event hosted top restaurants, food trucks, live music, and much more.

Tomorrow he would take her to the set where they were filming. He was not on-call for the session, but he thought Robin would be fascinated to see behind-the-scenes. At night, he planned to head them to the Hampton Court Palace Festival with a stunning line-up of singers, bands, dream-like settings, fireworks, and open-air bars. "Wait 'til you see the impressive open-air Tudor courtyard and beautiful East Gardens. You'll love it," Richard said happily, delivering a full agenda of activities. His bright eyes sparkled with joy.

Robin threw herself into his arms. "It's so wonderful to be here with you, Richard." "Okay leeetle Rrrrrobbbin, we will have a grand time."

That night, after the excitement of experiencing the Night Market, Robin crawled naked into Richard's bed waiting for him to join her. His body was warm and muscular as he nuzzled against her smooth, soft skin. Slowly he caressed her taut figure, running his hands gently over every inch, reacquainting himself with every part of her. Firm small breasts, flat tummy, beautifully rounded buttocks. She thrilled at his touch. He kissed her softly at first, nibbling on her lips, and then his tongue played with hers. She gazed intently into his eyes, the blueness of all the oceans of the world focusing on her and her alone. In a strong, graceful movement, he pulled her to him until they were entangled in such intense lovemaking that Robin felt an overwhelming sense of oneness, unable to discern what body parts were hers and what were his. Glorious ripples of energies overwhelmed all her senses and then it was over. Sprawled on their backs on the cool sheets, their bodies were beaded with perspiration and satisfaction. Richard carefully snaked his arm beneath her shoulders, and they dissolved quickly into exhausted sleep.

The visit was magical. Between sightseeing all over the city, dining at all kinds of places from fancy to casual restaurants and taking long walks in the parks, their lovemaking reached new levels of ecstasy. But throughout their two days, Robin could not contain her worries about Arles.

She expected that it was going to be odd being with her mother's friends and doing a re-creation of her disappearance. After all, so many years had passed, what did she think she would uncover? What if something terrible happened on this trip and it would be her fault for bringing everyone to France? And what if nothing happened and she left empty, with feelings unresolved? Richard listened and listened and listened. There were no answers, only exacerbated fears.

And then their time together was over, evaporating in seeming microseconds as Richard chauffeured Robin back to the airport. They embraced one last time. Robin stared into Richard's eyes hoping to find some reassurance in them, about their relationship, life, the future. But she found only a twinkling smile that almost felt ingenuine. She sensed that Richard had something to say, something to tell her. But he held back. Was she misreading the moment?

Old insecurities mushroomed like a nuclear cloud exploding in her mind and body. She wondered if Richard loved her. They never ventured into that territory of professing love for one another. They both enjoyed being together and accepted the deep affection they shared. But there was nothing more. Or was there?

A part of Robin's femaleness was now feeling hurt, taken, misled, even abused. After all the beautiful sex and connectedness, she now felt empty, like a vacuum had sucked her energies along with all recognition of who she was. When she was with Richard, she felt on top of the world. He was so stunningly handsome, and she was the woman he had chosen to be with. But it all seemed so fleeting now as she watched from her window seat on the plane as London shrank into a toy-like miniature.

Nan and Stephanie had arrived in Arles a day earlier, so they drove their rental to pick up Robin at the airport in Marseille. Once united, on the way to Arles, they were all quite pleased with themselves that the plan was coming together so far.

"We'll be there in about an hour," Nan advised and told Robin that she had reserved the same room at the Hôtel Nord-Pinus but there had been a few renovations over the last 25 years so it was not quite the same.

"But we still have a view of the famous Van Gogh Café," piped in Stephanie.

Even at 67, Nan was still an extremely attractive woman. Her blonde hair had turned silvery and was pulled back in a loose ponytail. Signs of age were obvious in her facial wrinkles, but they seemed to be more from smiles as she exuded a happy demeanor. She wore navy stretch pants and an oxford collared blue pin-striped shirt worn loosely, camouflaging her body. She had a stately and very natural look that belied her age.

Nan wanted to know about Robin's visit with Richard, to which Robin simply replied, "Nice. It was good to see him and to visit London." Nan asked when she thought he'd be returning to the States. Robin didn't want to talk about Richard right now and she answered more harshly than she intended that she really had no idea. Nan changed the subject and talked about how perfect the weather was expected to be during their stay.

Robin tried to be social by asking both Nan and Stephanie about their kids, who were grown and living full lives. Everyone was fine and seemed to be thriving. Nan had three adorable grandchildren that happily lived near her. Stephanie had one grandson who she spoiled and was encouraging into the artistic route, but he was more interested in science and math. They continued small talk until at last they pulled into Place du Forum and Robin saw the hotel.

"Wowie," she exclaimed.

"That's exactly what your mother said the first time we saw this place,"

Stephanie laughed at Robin's reaction to the impressive exterior. "Wait 'til you see inside." Stephanie was now 65 and had not aged well. She was severely overweight and all the years of carrying extra pounds had worn out her knees. Walking was painful and she knew she would need to face having at least one knee replacement if not two! She still favored artsy outfits and was wearing billowing harem pants topped with a long-sleeved cover-up designed with Monet's waterlilies. She looked and walked like an elderly lady and resembled a lumbering Buddha.

Entering their hotel room, both Nan and Stephanie stood back to watch Robin take in the scene. The antique chandeliers were dazzling, and the beds still had wrought iron frames like they had when her mother had been there. Robin sighed out loud, putting down her carry-on bag and heading to explore the terrace. The two sexagenarians followed so closely and silently that Robin almost collided with them as she whirled back around to re-enter the room. They all snickered. It was a Keystone Kop moment of silliness but simultaneously became a welcomed release. They all felt the weightiness of the moment and their nerves were frayed.

Nan was the first to speak about how difficult this experience was for everyone. "We need to support each other through this as best we can," Nan suggested.

Robin expressed gratitude to both women not only for being such amazing friends to her mom but also for being willing to step back into the moments before she vanished. Robin could not even begin to imagine what being here was like for them.

"Well let's not make it all emotional and no play," said Stephanie, trying to inject air back into the tenseness of the room. "I'm ready to hit the café. Any takers?" They all chuckled and agreed.

The rushed, sweaty waiter brought their drinks and placed them abruptly together in one spot on the table and left. Each of the three claimed their glass of red wine. As they sipped the *Cote du Rhone*, Robin showered Nan and Stephanie with endless questions. Did my mom like it here? Did she have a favorite place? What do you think she liked the best? Did she talk about my dad? About my sister? About me?

The conversation was animated with Nan and Stephanie being as forthright and as open as possible. Ruth had seemed very at home in Arles, they declared. She adored antiquity and how it was witness to centuries of human stories. She enjoyed Les Baux, the street markets, and had a fascination for the gypsies who squatted on the edge of town. But most of all, she was drawn to La Natura and its owner Marcel who was still there and expecting a visit from them.

"Let's go," urged Robin. "I'd like to meet Marcel."

As they meandered down the cobblestone streets, Robin could not take her eyes off the billowing vines of fragrant purple wisteria that decorated many of the building facades. She commented on how much she loved that look. So soft and elegant.

Nan and Stephanie stared at each other. Stephanie said, "Like mother, like daughter."

Stephanie told Robin how her mom was drawn to the wisteria.

"So breathtaking," Robin exclaimed.

"Your mom was planning to grow them on her house when she got back from the trip," said Nan.

"Really?" Robin looked thoughtful. "I think I could grow them in Naples. Maybe I'll do that…" Her voice trailed off.

The front of Marcel's bookstore-gallery still looked the same after all these years. The big blue shutters were opened as was the front door. They entered but no one was there. "*Bonjour,*" Nan called out loudly.

"Oh wow," exclaimed Robin. "I love this place." She felt an odd familiarity, an energy that made her feel at home.

"*Bonjour, un moment, s'il vous plaît,*" came a male voice from behind a door on the opposite side. Then an older, silver-haired man emerged with a quick step and a graciousness. At 58, Marcel had aged significantly but he still had a friendly warmth and a kindness infused in his eyes.

"Ah bonjour, mesdames." Marcel was animated and happy to see Nan and Stephanie. He greeted them by extending his hands to hold each of theirs and kissing each cheek. He turned to Robin, who felt a shudder down her spine as he said, "And you must be Ruth's daughter." He took both her hands in his and tilted his head as he eyed her up and down, like someone might appraise an object of sculpture they're considering purchasing. He kissed her cheeks side to side and then a third one in a show of keen affection.

Robin found herself blushing from Marcel's unusual attention. He offered everyone drinks and the ladies chose Perrier as they sidled up to the well-worn wooden bar. Marcel served the bubbling water in elegant wine glasses and moved a small, wrapped gift that had been in the middle of the polished countertop out of their way. Robin was surprised to feel such ease in this stranger's shop. She liked the antiquity of the vaulted arches. The gallery, while small, was quite lovely and the bookstore was so attractive that she couldn't resist wandering over to one of the tall built-in shelves to see what books he carried. Marcel chatted with Nan and Stephanie about all the years that had passed and how good it was to see them and meet Robin. Soon Robin was back on a stool with the others holding up a book as if it was a prize.

"I've always wanted to read this," she exclaimed. Everyone was shocked as she held *The Diary of Anaïs Nin,* Volume I. They all began talking about Ruth. As they discussed their bewilderment over her untimely disappearance, a sad expression came over Marcel. He took a deep breath and began to talk in detail about that day.

Marcel looked at Robin as if determining if she were ready to hear about her mother from a Frenchman she'd never seen before. He started to lose himself in the memories and plunged in, feeling like it had all just happened yesterday rather than over two decades ago. From the moment he had met Ruth, he seemed to find her incredibly special. There was a lightness and at the same time a depth and authenticity about her that he seemed to admire.

When Ruth came that day to pick up the book, he related, they connected in an uncanny, unspoken bond. Ruth intuited Marcel's feelings and his struggles with finances and his business.

At that time, he was trying to survive. He had invested all his savings in La Natura, and he had not been getting the traffic or sales to make ends meet. He had been dating a woman he desperately wanted to marry but couldn't even afford to think about asking her with his financial difficulties at the time.

Marcel looked deeply into Robin's eyes as she listened attentively.

When Ruth left that day, Marcel begged her to stay for another drink. He didn't want her to go. And then as if the gods had heard him, the skies opened with torrential, unrelenting rain and she came running back drenched to the bone and laughing that she guessed she wasn't supposed to leave yet. She stayed at least another hour to dry off and talk more about life… and loves.

Marcel paused to slow the emotions that seemed to overwhelm his senses. As weird as it sounded, Ruth had wanted him to know that she could see the future and that she knew he would make a big success here and he should propose to the woman he loved. To seal her prediction, she took off the silver locket that she always wore and gave it to him. She said she would come back someday and that he could return it to her when he was prosperous and happy.

"I refused to take it," cried Marcel. "She was so amazing. I believed her about the future, but I could not take her beautiful piece of jewelry. That was too much. Then she had to go as she knew you two would be worried since she'd been gone for so long." He looked intensely at Nan and Stephanie trying to gauge their reactions.

They were hanging on every word. Marcel had never told them any of this. He'd been afraid and confused with all the commotion at the time and the endless investigations and questions. He continued, explaining that Ruth had forgotten the way to the Forum. Pierre, his assistant, was leaving for the day so he offered to point her in the right direction.

"I hugged her," admitted Marcel. "I felt such an attachment to her." He stopped again and looked down at his glass before continuing.

"I know this will sound crazy but sometimes I see her here. She visits me, especially on days when it is raining heavily. She just hovers by the bookcase where you just were." He looked at Robin. "I was heartbroken when she vanished. The day after she disappeared, I was stocking a few new books on that same shelf and on the very edge…" Marcel paused again, choking back emotions as he reached for the small, wrapped gift. "She left this." He handed the tiny package to Robin. "I have guarded and cherished it for all these years…for you." His hand was shaking as he held it for Robin.

Robin hesitated and then accepted. "May I?," she asked, mimicking opening it.

"Mais oui," affirmed Marcel.

Robin felt a surge of emotions from anxiousness to anticipation. What had her mother given to Marcel?

She carefully opened the package and there, nestled in the thoughtfully chosen decorative blue paper with olive motifs like the scarf she loved from Les Baux, was her mother's beautiful silver locket. Nan and Stephanie gasped. Noticing a tiny hinge, Robin pushed her nail into the small indentation at the top outer edge. It popped open easily. On one side, behind slightly yellowing round plastic, was a picture of Robin, about age three, posing in front of her sister Jean. Robin wore a blue jumper and proudly displayed a sparkling plastic tiara sitting atop her dark straight hair. Jean, who was probably six, wore a ruffled white blouse and was grinning broadly, standing inches taller, her arm protectively tucked around her sister's shoulder. Slipped into the other side of the silvery jewel was a tiny, folded note. With trembling hands, Robin unfurled the pleated paper and read the words written in her mother's handwriting, "An open heart lets in light and love."–Uriel Emanuel.

Robin's shoulders began to heave, deep breaths transformed into sobs. "I'm sorry," she apologized between the tears. "I-I didn't expect this." It pained Robin to see the little sisters framed together in frozen happiness and how her mother was always holding that image against her heart. Did her mother live in the past? Did she ever understand how the relationship between the sisters had disintegrated so completely? Did her mother believe in the ideal of a supportive, loving family even though it had become a myth?

Nan and Stephanie, momentarily paralyzed, stared at Robin while Marcel wrapped his arms around her, forcing out waves of cathartic tears. Stephanie hurriedly rifled in her purse and handed Robin a packet of tissues. She dabbed at her eyes to mop up an endless stream of water.

"Everything your mother told me came true. My business became a big success. I married the woman of my dreams and we have two wonderful children. I never forgot Ruth and her prophecies and my special connection with her. I gave my daughter Michelle the middle name of Ruth. Your mother promised she would come back and here you are." Robin felt comforted by Marcel.

"I do not believe in death," stated Marcel. "Energy never dies. It only transforms."

Nan smiled at hearing the very same words she had said to Robin.

Marcel continued. "Your mother is here. In a different form. I can still hear her predictions from time to time. Thoughts just come into my head as if they are my own, but I know better. I know where they come from. I knew you would be coming soon."

Robin was so overcome by conflicting feelings of loss, discovery and joy that she could not speak. She felt a renewed connection with her mother. She knew only too well of her mother's psychic abilities which had haunted and helped her through those treacherous teenage years.

But when her mother vanished, the guidance was gone. And now, in some very strange turn of fate, her mother was communicating again. "Anytime you need answers to life's challenges," Marcel said, "she will give you what you need. I'm sure of it."

Stephanie gingerly took the note from Robin and read the quote again. She looked up with a puzzled expression. "Who the heck is Uriel Emanuel?"

No one had any idea. Marcel Googled him. "American-born entrepreneur, author and spiritual leader, Uriel Emanuel graduated from Harvard College and is 51 years old. His best-selling books are: *Psychic Answers from the Soul* and *A Compassionate Life* about spiritual awakening. He lives in New York City with his two golden retrievers and offers workshops all over the world on stepping into your power and connecting to your higher self."

"How did Ruth come across this guy? She never mentioned him. Gosh, what made her put that message in her locket?"

Robin calmed down to a soft sniffle. Indeed, who is Uriel Emanuel? What did all of this mean? She knew she needed to research more about this man who had obviously touched her mother enough for her to carry his message with her, next to a picture of her daughters.

When it came time to depart, Marcel hugged Robin for a long time and Robin surrendered. At the end she told him what a magical place he had and that she was so grateful to meet him and to know of his unique relationship with her mother.

Then she surprised herself when she added, "I will be back to visit in a few years with my husband." Marcel reacted with, "Oh I didn't know you were married."

Robin interrupted. "I'm not. But I will be, and I'll be back. At least, I'm feeling like I'll be back. I'm also getting this feeling like I need to meet your daughter with the middle name Ruth. I don't know. Maybe I'm just losing my mind."

Marcel smiled. "I will be happy for that time," he said with a knowing wink.

The three women said their goodbyes and walked out into the humid air of the day.

"That was crazy," exclaimed Robin caressing the locket she now wore proudly around her neck.

Stephanie gestured toward the silver piece. "No kidding. Just like Ruth to come back in a sneaky and bizarre way."

Nan pondered thoughtfully. Turning towards Robin, she said, "It did seem like Ruth was with us back there. Odd. Very odd."

"It feels nice." Robin smiled contentedly. "I like feeling her with me."

Falling into quiet contemplation, they strolled slowly so that Stephanie with her bad knees could keep up. But it seemed no one's feet were touching the ground as they floated their way back to their hotel in a tingly state of awareness.

Breaking the silence, Robin announced, "Now let's just enjoy our time in Arles. I have what I came for. There is nothing else I need to find."

"Except maybe this Uriel guy," Stephanie interjected jokingly.

Robin laughed. "Yeah, sure!"

They had a few more days and made the best of them. They visited Camargue. They wanted to see the trail of five gorges, but they were only accessible by bike or on foot and both choices were too daunting for Stephanie's knees. So, they opted for a three-hour guided safari tour with an organization that breeds horses and bulls in the Camargue.

As they rumbled along in a 4x4 jeep through a magnificent landscape of marshes and salt flats, their guide, Jean-Marc, explained the history, culture and wildlife. The white horses were majestic, and they got to see black bulls, graceful pink flamingos and even gypsies. Nan and Stephanie sighed deeply, thinking of Ruth's fascination with these colorful, nomadic travelers.

The wildlife was impressive with over 15 bird species. Enamored with the authenticity of their experience, they learned about the bull culture and the volunteer horsemen called *gardians*. The safari landed back at the starting point in the town of Aigues Mortes at 1 p.m. so they decided it was high time for lunch. They picked *Le Saint Amour*, a French-Mediterranean restaurant.

"How can you not want to stop at a place with a name that translates to Saint Love?," quipped Nan.

"Sounds like my kind of place," laughed Robin.

"Take me…," joked Stephanie.

Upon entering, they immediately liked the sleek, contemporary interior and open kitchen. But even more enchanting was the extremely attentive, warm, and very friendly servers. Robin ordered the fresh Mediterranean red tuna, Nan had the sliced leek with roasted scallops and Stephanie chose marinated royal salmon with seasonal vegetables. The food was well presented and sumptuous.

They chatted about the uniqueness of their experience and how fortunate that they had splurged on the jeep safari. They saw much more than they would have on their own, especially some of the private lands.

"I'm so awed by it all. I felt like a kid," gushed Robin.

"You are a kid," shot back Nan.

They all laughed and toasted with their glasses of mineral water.

"It's curious," Stephanie said. "I know I'm considered old and I have bad knees and high blood pressure…"

Nan interrupted with shock in her voice. "You have high blood pressure?"

Stephanie explained that it was not bad, and she was managing it. But even with all her ailments, she didn't feel old. In her mind, she was still that young 22-year-old bride who had just married her husband.

"It's that youthful artistic side of you," Nan suggested.

Robin looked pensive for a moment and then exclaimed in all honesty, "I still feel like a teenager." She paused. "It's one of the things I'm working on…figuring out how to grow up. I mean…ladies…you may not realize it but I'm a middle-aged woman."

Stephanie made a gagging sound as if she were throwing up.

"Try 67 on for size," said Nan, agreeing that self-perceptions of age are often distorted. "Some of my contemporaries look and act so old, I can't believe we even went to school together. But in fact, perceptions of time are often warped, too, don't you think?"

Stephanie jumped in with a thought about how it could be possible that 25 years had slipped by.

"Exactly," said Nan.

Robin quietly reflected. In all her years filled with risky adventures, especially motorcycling, Robin often struggled with the perception of both time and age. She was serious when she claimed she felt like a teen. It was as if her body were going through the aging process, but her mind refused to participate, and it would override any bodily limitations. She could "see" that she was getting older. She noticed how the backs of her hands were mapped with veins, and her thighs were no longer smooth and creamy but dotted with dark spots. Signs were there when she looked in the mirror: lines on her forehead, wrinkles at the corners of her eyes, hair beginning to gray. But while she was not enamored by all the physical clues, she had no sense of being too old to do all the things she wanted. Physically, she felt as if she had no boundaries, no restrictions, even after breaking several bones from her accident. She still felt that she could climb the highest mountain or scuba dive to the farthest depths of the ocean. How could she reconcile these feelings? she wondered to herself. Was it her soul—or a kind of consciousness—that remained ageless?

"I think age is a state of mind," she ventured. "You are what you think you are. I'm still 18, goddammit."

"You go girl," said Stephanie. "I must admit, there are days when my aches and pains make me feel like I'm 95 instead of 65."

Nan piped in that there was a recent scientific study that showed brains can age differently and influence how someone feels age wise.

"Oh, here she goes," joked Stephanie.

"No seriously. One was published in *Frontiers in Aging Neuroscience* and showed a link between subjective age, in how you perceive yourself, and brain aging. Using MRI brain scans, the study revealed that elderly people who feel younger than their age show fewer signs of brain aging. The findings suggest that if you're feeling old, you can improve your brain health with certain anti-aging practices."

Robin had to agree. "I've actually been doing articles about those kinds of studies," she said. Living in Naples, she explained that she'd been writing about the concept of the Blue Zones, since Naples was in the process of becoming one of these health-focused communities. The blue zones are geographic areas of the world where people live to be over 100 years effortlessly due to better lifestyle choices. The project identified nine elements that contribute to more vitality and longer lifespans, and possibly improved brain health.

"The elements are called the Power of 9," Robin reported.

"You've got my attention," Stephanie said. "What are they? Hell, who wouldn't want to feel younger?"

Robin briefly outlined some of the practices like down-shifting to de-stress, eating a more plant-based Mediterranean diet and only eating to 80% of fullness, finding your purpose, having a glass of wine at 5 p.m., belonging, putting families first, and moving naturally.

"The oldest people in the world don't go to gyms or run marathons, they live by farming or doing some kind of outdoor work," Robin finished. "I'll send you my articles. What's great about living in a Blue

Zones Project Community is that all these choices become part of the culture of the region. So, restaurants incorporate blue zones-inspired dishes and there are walking groups and informational workshops. Stuff like that. Healthy options have become more accessible."

"I may need to look for a new winter home in Naples," said Nan. "Very appealing."

Stephanie listened intently but could not stop herself from ordering the sugary chocolate mousse and pear caviar. "Maybe I'll only eat 80%," she jested, adding, "You know, in deference to the blue period."

Robin guffawed. "It's blue zones!"

"You're so naughty," said Nan. "But I'd love a taste. It's the least I could do to save you from yourself!"

The three got along seamlessly without any conflict until the final day. They had retraced almost all the steps Ruth had taken—at least that they knew of. They had been to Les Arenes, Les Baux, the outdoor market. They'd visited the edge of town, although there were no gypsies the morning they had sauntered to the shore of the Rhone. Of course, the highlight had been the first stop at La Natura and the visit with Marcel. And they had added an amazing trip to Camargue which Ruth had so wished to experience. But now the big question was how they wanted to spend their last day.

Stephanie wanted to see a few galleries, the *Réattu* museum, and hang out at cafés. Nan had her heart set on seeing the underground Cryptoporticus, the network of tunnels beneath Place du Forum constructed by the Greeks, plus the church and cloisters of *St. Trophime* off Rue de la Republique.

Robin didn't know what she wanted to do, maybe just stroll the streets taking in the day in its full glory. Against better judgment, they separated with a decision to meet at sunset for *Champagne Framboise* at the Jules César.

Robin enjoyed soaking in the Arlesian atmosphere as exhaustively as possible. She wandered aimlessly down meandering streets, absorbed by the sights and sounds. The Provencal lifestyle was in full array. She watched people passing her on the streets, some glued to their phones talking in loud voices while others walked at a determined pace. Still others rode by on bicycles and several young moms pushed carriages. Like her early days on the streets of New York's Greenwich Village, she wondered where each was going. Then her thoughts turned inward. Where was she going? What would unfold on this glorious day in the South of France where her mother had vanished?

She passed a small outdoor market and stopped for some fruit and a small bag of nuts. The Arles amphitheater was not far, and she fixed on it as her destination. Arriving at the rows of cool, stone steps, she climbed halfway up and sat on the hard surface surveying the view below while she enjoyed her snack. Suddenly a young boy in shorts and a tee shirt went bounding up the stairs screaming, *"Oh merde. Mon drone s'est écrasé là-haut."*

Robin turned to look where he was going and saw his toy drone in pieces at the top. *"Je t'ai dit de faire attention,"* an older boy bellowed clearly annoyed as he raced after him.

Robin smiled to herself thinking, "Shit happens. It's about risks and rewards. Or was it?"

Now she had risked finding out about her mother. She would probably never know the truth but at least she felt she had gained something, an understanding, a connection to a part of her mother. Maybe it was just a fragment of her energy, but she could feel it at La Natura. She could feel it when she was around Marcel. Without any conscious thought, she was on her feet walking, guided towards Rue du Refuge and La Natura for one more visit.

"Oh, mon Dieu," Marcel exclaimed at seeing Robin walk through his front entrance. *"Tellement content de te voir."* He rushed to her, kissing both cheeks and then another. He hugged her.

"Hello Marcel," Robin said softly, almost feeling weak-kneed. "I hope

I'm not disturbing you. I'm not sure why I'm here."

"I'm pleased to see you again. Did you bring your husband?"

Robin looked puzzled. She had forgotten her assertion that she would be returning with a husband she doesn't have.

"No. No. Just me. She added with a gleam in her eye. "That will be next time."

Marcel told her that she could not have come at a better time as his teenage daughter Michelle Ruth was coming to work in a few minutes. Robin seemed elated that she would get to meet the daughter who was her mother's namesake.

Acutely aware of her surroundings, Robin was thoroughly delighted by the smells inside La Natura, the cool moistness of the stone walls mixed with the sweet, musky smell of books and a wafting scent of coffee. Marcel offered Robin some espresso that he had just made, and she plopped down on one of the plush sofas near the bookshelves. Just as she did, an attractive dark-haired young girl with a pixie-ish look and a pink cast on her arm walked in. Marcel greeted her very affectionately. *"Quelle moment! Je te présente à l'américaine nous t'avons nommé d'après sa mère.* Michelle Ruth, please meet Robin Stevens."

"Very nice to meet you," said the young girl in a British-accented English.

Robin was thrilled to meet this 15-year-old who carried something of her mother even if only in name. She immediately asked about her cast. Michelle Ruth looked at her father sheepishly and admitted that she had taken his scooter without permission and had had an accident. She'd broken her arm. Robin laughed, as she felt an immediate bond with the youngster sharing her own drama of broken bones from a motorcycle accident. Robin wanted to know where she acquired her excellent English.

"From my dad. Then, I took a semester in London last year. I was an exchange student."

"How wonderful," Robin gushed, mentioning that she'd just been in London. Robin wanted to know all about Michelle Ruth and was thrilled to discover she was interested in writing. It was not yet clear what kind of writing was fascinating to her.

Right now, she was writing a chronicle of her younger brother's antics which she found amusing. Alexandre was only 12 but had a flair for the absurd and did the darnedest things like trying to take a selfie with a squirrel and subsequently getting attacked by the furry animal. Another time he did a backflip in class and accidentally knocked his teacher unconscious. The worst one was when he didn't want to do his chores and rode away on his bicycle for two days, leaving his parents frantic about his whereabouts. Marcel kept trying to interrupt the revealing tales of his son but to no avail. Michelle Ruth was on a roll.

"That's pretty crazy stuff," Robin admitted. "So, Michelle Ruth, what brings you here today?" The young girl explained that once a week she helped her father with re-stocking shelves and helped with whatever else was needed. Robin was impressed with what a responsible and mature teenager Marcel was raising.

Marcel finally cut through their chatter with an invitation to dinner. "My wife makes the best bouillabaisse. Please join us tonight for dinner." Robin was touched by the invitation but explained that she was meeting Nan and Stephanie for their last sunset at the Jules César. Michelle Ruth looked disappointed.

Robin suggested that they stay in touch the old-fashioned way by writing letters. It would be a good exercise and would maintain a fun dialogue. And who knows, maybe she'd be interested in another student exchange program, this time in the United States. They could certainly work something out.

The energy was electric with excitement between Robin and the teenager as they discussed the future. Marcel interrupted and beckoned his daughter to bring him the top box off the new inventory that had just arrived in the back room. Obediently she followed his directions and came back with a medium-sized cardboard box that Marcel immediately tore open.

"This just came in and there's something for you," he announced to Robin. He paused as he pulled out a paperback book. He opened the cover, grabbed a pen from his shirt pocket, and wrote the date along with an inscription:

Chère Robin,
Puisse-tu connecter à ta sagesse intérieure comme le faisit si bien ta mère. [May you connect to the wisdom within, like your mother could.]

Chaleureusement,
Marcel

As he gave her the book, she was stunned to see the title: *Psychic Answers from the Soul* by Uriel Emanuel. Robin touched the silver locket she wore since Marcel had given it to her. In the book was the quote her mother had copied. Another gift from Marcel. Or was it from her mother? Was it synchronicity or destiny? A chill rippled up Robin's spine.

On the drive back to Marseille, Nan asked Robin if she had closure. Robin was feeling odd but in an okay kind of way. The trip had been surreal on many levels. Neither her mind nor words—even as a writer— could truly encapsulate this moment. Even though there was still a deep sadness that her mother was physically gone and that she would always miss her hugs and her expressions of approval or disapproval, she felt a new opening and a new way of being with her mother. She had a new attachment to her mother that she could have for the rest of her life. There was a certain solace in that understanding.

"I'm not sure I would call it closure," said Robin. "But I know what I need to know for now. How about you two? Are you content with the experience we've had?"

Stephanie answered first, admitting that she felt as if she were visiting her younger self throughout their visit. As they experienced familiar places, she could remember exactly her moods and reactions in each location. Yet those sensations were quiet, almost calming devoid of the panic of those last few days from the unsettling past.

Nan's view was somewhat similar. Time passing had contributed to healing the gaping wound and the awful despair caused by Ruth's disappearance. Nan would always miss her, but this trip had brought back many of the happy memories of their travels together. "Your mother was a quiet pistol," said Nan.

"Hmmm...which means?," asked Robin

Nan explained that Ruth had an insatiable curiosity for human stories, but she went about her explorations in a very subtle, almost misleading way. Nan wouldn't be surprised if she had been kidnapped by the gypsies and never tried to escape because their lifestyle was so compelling and fascinating.

Robin was lost in thought as they passed the outskirts of a biodiverse reserve, a protected territory of natural beauty, local plants and animals with all their fragility. Life is so tenuous, she thought. Blurs of color flew by the window, reminding her of the colossal floral arrangement at her father's funeral.

Three years after her mother's disappearance, Teddy Stevens died unexpectedly of a stroke. One minute, he was strong and healthy, the next, he was dead, supposedly alone at home. But it had been a woman who had called 9-1-1. Who knows? Maybe he always needed a woman and never got over the loss of his wife.

Robin remembered before the service, staring into the casket in disbelief. Her dad, clothed in his finest suit, looked more like a wax figure at Madame Tussauds than her father. No movement. No sounds. No raising or lowering of the chest. No heart beating. Just a still body, empty of the personality that gave it animation. Gone. She'd thought about what her mother might've looked like in a casket, wondering if her mother could still be alive somewhere.

At the funeral, amid her sad musings in front of her father's dead body, Jean abruptly jerked her away. She grabbed her arm forcefully and pulled her back. It hurt, both physically and emotionally. When she turned to her sister for comfort, Jean, with red rimmed eyes from crying, just motioned harshly for her to sit as the service was beginning.

As Nan drove the route through Salon de Provence, Robin descended deeper and deeper into thoughts about Jean, wishing she had some relationship with her sister, her only sibling. The last of her immediate family. Ever since Jean had returned from college, they had completely disconnected, strangers. She asked Nan and Stephanie if they had been in touch with Jean at all.

Stephanie said she hadn't. Nan was pensive at first, gathering courage to talk about Jean. She conceded that she had been in touch quite regularly. In fact, she had recommended a psychiatrist just a few years ago.

Robin asked, "Really? Why?".

Nan began to disclose the sorrowful story about Jean. "I guess it's time you know about your sister." Robin froze, not uttering a sound, expecting something cataclysmic, like an asteroid falling on the car exploding them all into oblivion. Or maybe that's what she wished would happen. Robin could feel anxiety and fear swelling her brain, sending stress hormones to activate drum-like heart palpitations. She leaned forward from the back seat to hear Nan more clearly through the deafening pounding in her chest.

Nan wasn't sure where to begin. "Your mom and dad conceived Jean before they were married. In fact, it forced them to marry and regrettably your mom had to drop out of college. While Ruth had always wanted children, she felt burdened by her unplanned pregnancy and cheated in her life. Three years later when you were born, your mom was ecstatic and filled with joy. You were expected and welcomed. As hard as your mother tried to overcome her resentment of your sister's arrival, she didn't mask it very well. As an unfortunate consequence, Jean felt unwanted and unloved whereas you were the chosen one, the favored child."

"I-I didn't know or feel that," Robin whispered.

Nan continued. "When Jean went off to college, she was seeking love in all the wrong places and made some really bad choices. She had sex with some hooligan, as your mother described the boy, and got pregnant. Your mom wanted to protect Jean. She didn't want her to have to endure what she had gone through in such a life-altering experience of having a baby…and out of wedlock. Your father never knew about any of this. In fact, no one knew except me."

"Because I was married to a doctor, your mother contacted me about finding somewhere that Jean could have a safe abortion. But Jean was impetuous. Instead, she ran away with her unsuitable boyfriend who found an illegal abortion clinic. A butcher did the job. He was so unskilled that the operation rendered Jean unable to ever have any children. After that, Jean was never the same. You were only 16 at the time and I know many times your mother wanted to tell you about Jean but could never find the right way. You and Jean had been so sisterly before that time but after such a trauma, Jean became distant and depressed. And she refused to let you—or anyone—know anything. We thought things would change when she met and married Nathan. He's exceedingly kind but truly he's just enabled Jean to stay rooted in her shell of denial. So, all these years have taken a toll."

The car was as silent as a snowflake in the night.

Robin digested the account of her sister's regretful life. Jean didn't deserve the hand she was dealt. How did Robin become a gift while Jean had been her parent's burden? A child is a child is a child. She vowed to reach out to Jean. She had no idea what would come of it but at least she would try with a new understanding and purpose. She was determined to open the lines of communication.

CHAPTER NINE

*R*obin was glad to return to the tropical paradise of Naples. In the last seven days, she had lived lifetimes and was more than exhausted from traveling and dealing with all the bizarre revelations. Her overactive brain was still whirling like a salad spinner getting every drop of water off the lettuce. She was too tired to digest or even manage all her thoughts. As she entered her condo, it seemed changed; the lighting was more subdued, the rooms more cramped. It looked and felt different. No one had been there. Nothing could have been altered. The reality was that she had changed and was in an unfamiliar state of mind. She felt as if she'd been rocketed into the cosmos and had returned through a tunnel of light that changed how she perceived her world.

She took off her shoes and sat cross legged on her cocoa leather couch gazing out at the lake, its fountain spewing rays of water that vibrated with reflections. Her carry-on travel bag was still packed and stood on the carpet in front of her like a silent soldier waiting on the front line. She took a full deep breath and let go with a sigh.

I'm home, she thought. She felt the silver locket around her neck, caressed it in her hands, and opened it. The folded paper fell out. She gazed at the words: *An open heart lets in light and love.* –Uriel Emanuel. The tiny picture of herself with her sister stared out at her from the silver background. A long-lost past.

Suddenly she was startled by the sounds of "bzzz" as her phone became animated, bouncing on top of her wooden coffee table like a jumping bean.

"Judy, I just got in," she said into the phone.

Judy suggested meeting for dinner.

"Come over and let's order take-out. I just want to be home." She was travel-weary and wanted to get reacclimated with the life she'd left a week ago, the life that now seemed removed by a dimension or two.

While waiting for Judy, Robin unpacked and found the book Marcel had given to her, *Psychic Answers from the Soul*. She began reading about how your soul is always in communication with your being and that it takes practice to develop awareness, to tune in and see the light of your spiritual path. With regular practice, the book advises, you go deeper into your soul, connecting to your higher self. And you release bubbles of intuition that you can trust more and more to create an opening for your divine presence and immense greatness to shine through. Emanuel writes, "You are so much more expansive than you know. Trust in this process. The experience feels mystical and yet it is part of your oneness with a cosmic, universal source of energy. When you bring mind and body into union, creating alignment, you transcend from three-dimensional reality to a quantum field of infinite energies and possibilities. Surrender and you will discover magic and miracles."

A jarring ring pierced her concentration, almost catapulting her to the floor. Her heart launched into overdrive, pumping stress hormones into her body. Realizing it was the doorbell, she trundled down the stairs to greet Judy, who was toting bags emitting delicious smells from *Café Nutesse*.

"Sheesh, I never realized how loud that bell is," said Robin, laughing.

Hugging awkwardly while trying to help with the shopping bag of steaming foods, Robin realized she was starving. Quickly arranging table settings and tearing into the entrees, the two friends were soon consuming the culinary delights along with amazing stories.

A nighttime glow lit up the fountain in the lake beyond the windows and inside the soft lighting of the dining room chandelier along with a Himalayan salt lamp radiating in the corner gave the place a cozy touch. In the background, soothing meditation music gave a relaxing and pleasant aura to her home.

Robin ooed and ahhhed at the delicious tastes while she recounted details of the trip. Judy listened intently without interruption. She adored Robin and genuinely wanted the absolute best for her. Occasionally, she acknowledged to Robin, she felt a flicker of jealousy as Robin's life seemed full of excitement and experiences. Even though some were traumatic, she said she envied Robin's ability to get involved in fun relationships after her divorce. And Richard was smart, sexy and a looker. How could Judy avoid battling the twinge of longing for someone special?

Judy seemed to push away the uncomfortable feelings of jealousy and longing. She had spoken to Robin about those old patterns from her nursing days when her emergency room duties were exhausting. In those days, she'd return home in the evenings to her tiny cottage on the outskirts of town so bone tired that she'd fall asleep often without taking time to have dinner and sometimes not even taking off her clothes. A relationship would have been nice, she said, but her responsibilities left little time for socializing, never mind finding a caring partner. That took time and effort, neither of which she had.

An attractive blonde, always dressed in yoga clothes that revealed her slim body, Judy exuded a comfortable confidence that blossomed and filled a room which drew people to her. The take-charge nursing background combined with the softness of her new venture gave her a friendly, balanced yin-yang presence in almost all situations. She seemed content with her life, not that there weren't areas that she could work on, but she was enjoying the fullness of her work. More importantly, she said she felt like she was making even more of a difference than when she was a nurse.

Now she had the time to date but her devotion to the Golden Moon store was a priority. Not many guys were interested in essential oils or gemstones. She had a lovely cadre of women friends that she'd cultivated. Of course, Robin was her closest and dearest among them. But dating didn't seem to fit into her lifestyle. Off limits was the idea of meeting someone over the internet. "I need to look in someone's eyes and be able to touch them. You can't do that through a computer," she complained about online dating sites. So instead she'd lose herself in research about new healing modalities or attend workshops about everything from nutrition to personal development to gemstone and aromatherapy. She'd begun to fabricate her own unique blends of essential oils at Golden Moon for people needing support for sleep, stress, trauma, and pain. Custom blends were her specialty for clients who appreciated her attention and compassion, and she was getting good at it. If only she could create an essential oil to attract a guy for herself. But in the end, it didn't matter. She was thoroughly enjoying her life.

Judy pushed away her empty plate. Her attention was fully on the book Robin had gotten from Marcel which she was glancing through with abundant curiosity. She paused, laid the book on the table, picked up her phone and Googled the author.

"He looks really interesting," Judy commented, reading all about this bright and intriguing man. "And hey look, he's doing a weekend workshop in Miami next month."

"Really!" Robin exclaimed sarcastically, as if Judy was making this up.

"Really! I'm not kidding you," Judy asserted excitedly.

"What are the chances…"

Judy interrupted, "I think we should go."

The synchronicity was mind-boggling. A week ago, they'd never heard of this guy and now she and Judy were plotting to attend one of his programs. Judy convinced Robin to be open to new possibilities. "You can pray for guidance and meditate only so much. When the universe sends you signals and a roadmap to follow, you need to heed the directions."

"You're being sent this guy and his transformational work. Heck, your mother sent him…"

"Sheesh. This is insane."

"It's obvious to me," said Judy. "Miami is the next destination and let's see what will unfold for you there."

Robin was used to Judy's impromptu fortune telling yet she couldn't help but reflect on how bizarre the timing seemed to be. On the contrary, Judy saw it as logical.

"This guy probably gives lots of workshops in Miami, but he was never on our radar before, so we didn't connect with him. It's like when you bought your baby blue Sportster…"

Robin cringed, remembering that she planned to sell it.

"That color and model had been around for years, but you didn't really notice it until you had yours. Then suddenly you were seeing your same bike all over the roads and at rallies. Before then, it wasn't in your conscious awareness."

Robin agreed. "So true. Much exists in the world that we only see a fraction of, even when it's right in front of us."

Judy tapped on Emanuel's book as if it held all life's answers. "We have selective perceptions, only noticing a bigger view when something changes within us to expand our consciousness. It's like scientists standing on the shoulders of previous scientists to see further, discover more, expand and progress." "It's called 'personal growth'," said Robin.

"Or is it evolution?" Judy pondered.

"Sure, let's go to what's his name's thing," Robin declared. She had an assignment to do a story about the art district in Miami for *Art Life* magazine and could combine those efforts and maybe get some expenses covered.

"And now, what about your sister?" Judy prodded.

Robin swallowed hard. Her relationship with Jean was difficult at best and now knowing the truth about Jean that Nan had shared made it even more complicated. She was soliciting advice from Nan on how to reach out to her sister. So far, they had not come up with any viable ideas. But it was a work in progress and something Robin felt committed to pursuing. It would happen. She would get quality time with Jean, she just didn't know when or how.

Judy asked with genuine wonder, "And how was your visit with Richard?" She may not have known she opened another can of worms that Robin did not want to delve into at this moment. Robin still wasn't sure what she'd felt when leaving Richard. Was she just being needy, wanting some assurance that they even had a relationship? She was still processing the entire episode, trying to figure out where she stood. She deflected the conversation by suggesting they call it a night. Jet lag had fried her brain and she needed some rest.

Judy was understanding but before she took her leave, she surprised Robin with a small gift advising her to use it before bed. It was a small brown vial of a special essential oil blend that Judy had created just for Robin. She called it "Oils of Intuition," consisting of lavender, frankincense, rose, and neroli. It would help open her pineal gland.

"I'm not sure I'm ready," Robin said in a way that signaled a withdrawal from the conversation. All the traveling coupled with talking about the unusual experiences was draining both physically and emotionally. It was as if all her energies were suddenly emaciated, drained by gravity, leaving her empty and desperately needing quality sleep.

Robin knew about the pea-sized pineal gland located near the hypothalamus and pituitary gland. In her yoga training, it was recognized as the third eye. The physical eye can see the physical world. Third eye activation opens to a higher consciousness and brings abilities linked to lucid dreaming, astral projection, improved sleep, and expanded imagination. Robin knew that humans are spirit beings in physical bodies, but at this moment every fiber of her physical body needed to lie down and rest.

She left the remainder of the unpacking for the morning and dabbed Judy's liquid essential oils under her nose, added a drop to her pillow, and pulled the covers tightly around her. She was feeling sated and peaceful as she closed her eyes and instantly disappeared into a deep sleep.

Suddenly she was aware of a presence in the room. Someone was staring at her, standing right next to the king-sized bed that was overflowing with fluffy pillows. Robin could feel the energy of a person but while startled, she felt no panic. The moment yielded almost a sedative, calming effect. Her eyes felt glued shut as she worked them open enough to see who was in her bedroom.

Robin shrieked, her mouth remaining open in utter surprise. "Mom!," she yelled. Ruth Stevens looked exactly as she had 25 years earlier. She had a cute pixie hairstyle and an animation in her eyes that held both enthusiasm and wisdom. She quieted Robin with a long "Shhhhhh," as if telling a bedtime story to a little girl and not wanting her to miss the important part. She was wearing very colorful clothes that reminded Robin of the French gypsies.

Taking a slow, calculated breath, Ruth told Robin not to be alarmed. Robin was awake enough to know her mother could not be there talking to her and yet there she was. Ruth looked and sounded very real. Her face was luminous and smiling, crinkling the corners of her warm eyes. It was as if Robin were aware of what was happening but was feeling ethereal, in some other dimension. The atoms of matter were changing before her eyes. She sat up straight in her bed and begged her mother to explain what had happened. Slowly waving her right hand across her face as if erasing all the years, she told Robin that what happened wasn't important, to let go of the past.

"Just remember how much I will always love you, little one," she said convincingly. "And I will always love your sister."

"I love you too, mom." Robin was feeling tears welling up in her eyes.

"It is time for you to live," she told Robin. "Truly live. Get out of your head, little one." She urged Robin to open her heart so that she could see the bigger world that awaited her, the one full of rainbows and happiness.

"I've missed you so much." Robin reached out and wrapped her arms around her mother's petite body, giving her a mighty hug. Robin wept, eyes blurred by tears, her head buried in the softness of her mother's breast. She stayed there for what seemed like an eternity. As she got control of her emotions, Robin opened her eyes, releasing her arms which she quickly realized were tightly squeezing a jumbo pillow.

"Nooooooo," Robin yelled as she noticed the glowing red numbers on her digital clock were lined up at 3:33.

That was so real. She felt like 20 years old all over again.

Despair about her mother's disappearance now permeated every cell in her body. The years had slipped into decades. Through it all, there was always a tiny sliver of light; hope that her mother would be found. She would reappear. Robin could not accept that she was gone forever. And for a fleeting moment, she was back. She was standing beside Robin's bed talking to her.

Oh crap. I'm crazy.

Robin began reflecting on the bliss of her early childhood, the times spent together as a family. She remembered evenings hunkered down in front of the TV. They laughed at the bumbling detective Inspector Gadget, adored the futuristic utopian painted by the Jetsons, and marveled at the Depression-era Virginia family, The Waltons, who lived in the Blue Ridge Mountains.

When she was 11, while engrossed in a rerun about John-Boy and his family, her mother got a brilliant idea to take a trip to the Waltons' Blue Ridge Mountains. She decided on a three-day Columbus Day weekend in October. Neither her husband, Teddy, nor Jean, who was 14, had any interest, so Ruth whisked Robin off to a sprawling mountain retreat, a six-hour drive from home and situated near the middle of Shenandoah National Park. The two of them stayed in a pinewood cabin which afforded them exquisite views of the Shenandoah Valley and the Blue Ridge Mountains.

Getting there had been a challenge.

Never good at directions, Ruth had taken them off the road more than once, bumping along narrow stone and dirt single lane paths bordered by curtains of trees. When the road widened enough, Ruth carefully turned the car back around each time.

Unfortunately, the detours significantly delayed their arrival. The sun had long set by the time they navigated the winding road to their cabin. In pitch-black darkness, Ruth attempted to work the code on the cabin's key box. She hadn't thought about bringing a flashlight, so she tried to position the car's headlights toward the front door, but the elevation of the road was too far below the entrance. She and Robin were weary and hungry, but still managed to laugh about their plight. They had a cooler of food they were planning to cook but now they couldn't even get in.

Robin reminded her mom that they'd passed a house with lights on at the beginning of the switchback road. Piling back in the car, Ruth took them down the steep, hazardous road, gripping the steering wheel so tightly that she lost feeling in her fingers. With trepidation and embarrassment, she pulled into a stranger's gravel-stone driveway. A tall burly guy, maybe in his thirties, bounded out the door of a log cabin, more than willing to help the damsels in distress. Muscular with a beer belly hanging over his shorts, the tough-looking man wore heavy hiking boots as he crunched his way to his pickup truck motioning for them to follow.

Ruth commented under her breath about their luck finding Paul Bunyan and what a spectacle he displayed on this cold night in his shorts and boots! His powerful flashlight, which could've been seen all the way to the next state, did the trick and they finally entered their rustic weekend accommodations.

"Home at last," Ruth exclaimed when they were alone. Robin just hugged her mom which made everything perfectly fine.

During the days, they hiked sections of the Appalachian Trail through the well-marked Skyland and Big Meadows areas. They were glad they had bought rugged boots for their adventures as they navigated through rocky terrain. Each wore a small backpack with water and snacks which they'd stop to enjoy along the way. The multicolored leaves of fall against the blues of the mountains provided awe-inspiring scenery. Ruth was impressed with the beauty and condition of the side trail, especially the side trails to the 4,050-foot summit of Hawksbill Mountain and Crescent Rock.

Ruth knew about the history of the area from reading books. The first traces of humans to the area dated back more than 8,000 years ago when Native Americans visited to hunt and gather food around these granite peaks which were formed a billion years earlier. In the late 1800s, city dwellers escaped to the mountains for much-needed respites from urban life, enticed by majestic views, fresh water and cool breezes.

As they hiked at their own comfortable pace, Ruth and Robin relished the cool temperatures in the mid-fifties. Robin was happily snuggled into a hooded sweatshirt, while Ruth wore a red and black flannel shirt that would be appropriate on a deer hunter but overwhelmed her small frame. She told Robin the story of the entrepreneurial and charismatic George Freeman Pollock, Jr., who created the legacy of Skyland and called the stunning views "beauty beyond description." Robin loved hearing stories as her mother infused each tale with an animation and zestiness that made the entire area endearing.

In the evenings, they would make dinner together, then relax on the rocking chairs of their private deck and watch the orange ball of sunlight slide behind the mountaintops, which rapidly dropped the temperature. For Robin, this was a special time with her mom, who gave undivided attention and shared her own thoughts and perceptions of the moment. It made Robin feel like a grown up.

The changing fall colors enchanted Ruth, but at the same time made her sad as they signaled the life and death cycle of nature and the coming of a cold, snowy winter. But, she insisted to Robin, the immediate moment was something to remember and enjoy again and again. In that way, death is never tragic, just part of the cycles of life.

"Let this moment be a reminder of the immense beauty and love that exists. Look at that." She gestured toward the stately trees and vast mountain range as they sat outside.

Ruth turned to Robin and in a sweet voice said, "I love you, little one." Robin's quality time with her mother gave her more maturity than the average kid her age. Her mother encouraged her to pause and cherish each experience as it unfolded.

As Robin lay in her warm bed all these years later, she smiled at the distinctive memory but felt disturbed by her mother's eerie bedside visit. Very strange, she muttered to no one. Her heart was still thumping loudly, feeling like it might explode out of her chest. After a glass of water and several slow cleansing breaths, she dabbed another drop of Judy's magic potion under her nose, and promptly fell asleep.

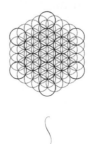

CHAPTER TEN

*T*he morning sunlight streamed through Robin's bedroom windows as she opened her eyes, glancing outside to see gently swaying palm trees and blue skies. She luxuriated in the fact that she was at last in her own bed. It felt so good to be home. She could hear the melodies of birds greeting the day. Then, like a bolt of lightning, she remembered the shock of last night. Was she nuts? Thoughts swirled reminding her of the weird night visitation of her mother. What was that?, she wondered, and felt a shudder surge through her body.

Before even getting out of bed to pee, she threw her legs over the side, sat up straight at the edge, and closed her eyes. She laid her hands in her lap, palms up touching her thumb and index fingers together. She felt a strong desire to begin the day with a brief meditation to quell her reaction to the phantom sight of her mother. *I rest in calm awareness to embrace this beautiful day with my whole being*, she recited to herself. She watched the rising and lowering of her chest, noticing each lengthened inhalation and exhalation. Her back was straight, chin parallel to the floor. *Feel the energies*, she told herself. *Just be present with what is. Create an easy relationship with thoughts.*

She planted her tongue on the roof of her mouth behind her upper teeth and focused her attention on the third eye, instructing herself to drop into stillness.

In her yoga training, she had learned that "stillness leads to seeing." By quieting the mind, she entered the flow of knowingness. Internally, she knew many of life's truths, but past experiences and perceptions prevented her from seeing more and her heart had slammed shut. Her mother's apparition at her bedside motivated her to connect to a greater place of wisdom and understanding. She was enjoying the meditation when her phone announced in a robotic female voice, "Your friend is trying to reach you on your cellular device." She had created a special ringtone for several of her closest peeps, and this was the one for her designer friend, Suzanne.

Robin laughed to herself as she answered the call. Suzanne was effervescent in welcoming Robin home. She invited Robin to join her for a quick beach walk.

"I know it's still early," said Suzanne. "But I'd love to see you and you know it's an awesome way to start any day."

"For sure! I can meet you in 30 minutes," Robin responded without hesitation.

Suzanne and Robin met at their favorite starting point at the west end of 5th Avenue South in downtown Naples and walked towards the Naples Pier, a site that is on the National Register of Historic Places. The wooden structure, which extends about 1,000 feet into the Gulf of Mexico, was first built in the late 1880s but was rebuilt five times as the result of hurricane damage. The walkway was the perfect place to watch sunset, fish, or see frolicking dolphins and pelicans. The old relic was an iconic visual that represented the area.

It was just 8:30 a.m. so the pier and sandy white stretch of beach were mostly deserted except for an occasional jogger or fellow fitness walker, and clusters of terns, gulls and pelicans. Occasionally, an egret or blue heron would stand in the shallow waters.

The temperatures were getting warmer as the summer months approached but walking along the Gulf of Mexico still offered cooling breezes and sloshing barefoot through the sea waters was refreshing. The temperature was in the low eighties, but the humidity was high, so it felt a lot hotter. The sky was an unending dome of blue, a clear day when it was hard to find a single white cloud to mar the scene.

Suzanne wore one of her casual designs: white shorts with a blue hem landing mid-thigh and a matching sleeveless blue shirt with a white mandarin collar and a floppy, wide-brimmed white sun hat. Robin could see herself in Suzanne's mirrored sunglasses. Robin wore black Columbia shorts, topped with a light fluorescent green tee shirt and a matching green baseball cap. She had on Maui Jim sunglasses that made the colors in the landscape look even more saturated. Suzanne shared updates on some of the new outlets for sales of her casual wear designs and Robin talked about her experiences in Europe.

They strolled in the soft sand at the edge of the shore, stepping around shells and fish debris. They walked past the pier to the Port Royal neighborhood where homes ranged from 10,000-square foot beachfront structures at $60 million to bayfront spreads for a mere $7.5 million. They chatted about how crazy it was that wealthy people tore down multimillion-dollar homes to build their own personalized fantasies for even more millions. And they only occupied these architectural masterpieces for a few weeks every year. But that's Naples, where there are more millionaires than anywhere else in the world. Suzanne and Robin kidded about how more expensive homes just delivered more extensive responsibilities. They agreed that money never buys happiness and that owning things are not as important as real friends and close family.

Robin considered telling Suzanne about her weird nighttime experience with her ghostly mother but decided against it. She didn't want Suzanne to think she was mentally unstable, and she wasn't sure herself if she was sane or not at this point. Instead she talked about the situation with her sister Jean.

Suzanne's simple advice was to go see her. "Don't wait for a special occasion, make it a special occasion and just ask if you can come visit. The worst she can say is 'no,' right?"

"I suppose," was Robin's unconvincing response as she watched the waves lap gently onto the silky white sand. The Gulf looked calm as a lake. It had a brownish tinge from the runoff of mangroves, the shrubs that grow along the coast and leak tannic acid like tea bags, turning the salt waters brackish.

"You need to break the ice and take a chance," said Suzanne. "Call her and ask if you can come visit." "Sound advice," said Robin. "I'll think about it."

Robin always appreciated Suzanne's friendship, but she refrained from sharing all the details about her mother, Marcel, his daughter, or anything about her mother's interest in Uriel Emanuel. Robin reflected that different friends fulfilled different needs and right now walking the beach with Suzanne talking about the wealthy residents of Naples was enough. Robin didn't think she was withholding information but rather she edited what she believed Suzanne could relate to. She didn't feel that Suzanne would have any comfort level discussing psychic or spiritual matters. As a former science writer, Suzanne was more about concrete facts, black and white. To her, all the other stuff was hocus pocus and couldn't be proven.

Robin knew that science had quantified some of the previously considered esoteric beliefs like heart-brain coherence, energy healing, mental telepathy, reading brainwaves, and brain-to-brain interfaces. More exciting breakthroughs in neurosciences had shown how brain plasticity allows new, healthier patterns of behaviors to be developed. So, Robin knew, no one should feel stuck with their bad habits unless they want to be.

Robin's mind flashed on an article she had read, "You Are Not Your Genes," about epigenetic science revealing that no one must be enslaved by their genes. One might have a genetic propensity for cancer or heart attacks, but lifestyle choices can influence what genes turn on or off. A life of stress and anxiety deplete and undermine the immune system, turning on an unwanted gene expression like diabetes or lymphoma. Mitigation techniques such as meditation, mindfulness, yoga and emotional freedom technique (EFT) have become more commonplace, often spearheaded by spiritual leaders. Robin was glad to know many of these techniques but chastised herself for not applying what she knows.

It had been a decade since Suzanne had researched or written about any of these scientific discoveries. Understandably, she had been more absorbed in designing her successful women's line of golf clothing and was knee-deep in the marketing.

Robin always felt uplifted by walking the beach and noted to herself that she needed to do this more often with or without a friend by her side. She gazed out into the Gulf, wondering about the unknown, all the mysteries of life. She had great respect for nature in its simplicity and complexities. She appreciated the ecosystem and the refuge it gave her to feel more in harmony with the earth, to connect to a dimension beyond herself.

The feeling of communion she experienced filled her up energetically and raised her vibrations. It brought her an awareness of something greater and more powerful, something beyond imagination or comprehension.

"Where'd you go?" Suzanne broke into Robin's daydream, retrieving her from another world.

"I'm here. Just noticing…everything."

Suzanne smiled. They headed back. Suzanne had to return to work and suggested they have dinner together soon. Robin nodded enthusiastically in agreement.

Back at her condo, Robin entered her home office to tidy up and review her list of assignments and deadlines. She had decorated the office in muted colors that were a distinct contrast to the rest of her home so that when she entered her office, it gave a different vibe that settled her into a work state of mind. She still had a week before she needed to submit her article about sound therapy. She'd already done quite a bit of research before her trip but still had a couple of interviews to complete. Her research revealed that all matter vibrates at specific frequencies and that sound or vibration has a strong impact upon matter.

She wished that the scientist Dr. Masaru Emoto were still alive so she could interview him. He documented proof that human words, thoughts, sounds, and intentions change the molecular structure of water. Using Magnetic Resonance Analysis technology and high-speed photography, he demonstrated how water exposed to loving compassionate words resulted in beautiful molecular formations in the water while water exposed to fearful, ugly words delivered disfigured and unpleasant formations. She had his book, *The Hidden Messages in Water*. Imagine how words we casually toss around can profoundly impact someone negatively. As a writer, Robin was extremely mindful of her word choices.

She still had two sound experts to talk to and planned to set up interviews tomorrow. In the meantime, she checked her email. Right at the top was one that took her aback. It was from Richard. The subject line said: Forgive me!

She hesitated, not wanting to open it. She had a sinking feeling in her gut. But click on it she did and began reading the exceedingly long email. As she read it, she could hear Richard's charming French accent, but the message was depressing.

He had hoped to return to Naples so that he could tell her in person. He felt guilty for not confessing the truth when they were together in London. He professed to think the world of Robin and always wanted her in his life. But he had met someone in Paris and while he wasn't sure even a week ago where it was going, it was now a real relationship. His lover's name was Robert. They had some modeling gigs together.

Robin got stuck on the name. Robert? He's with someone named Robert??? Oh crap. Son-of-a-bitch. How could I not have known that handsome hunk was bisexual? A wave of anger spread through her body. Suddenly the air in her office was like liquid cement and had reached a boiling point. Robin released the invisible band she felt constricting her chest and sucked in a deep breath.

She flopped off her chair and landed on the soft beige carpet with a thud. Lying on her back, she glared at the ceiling trying to tame her emotions. She couldn't read the rest of the email and, anyway, what did it matter what else he had to say. They were done. It was over. He didn't love her and now he was with a guy. She felt betrayed.

She slowly got up and grabbed her phone. She called Judy, who expressed surprise to hear Robin hyperventilating. How could so much have happened in the short span since she'd left Robin just last evening? Robin told her about her mother's appearance during the night and the Dear John she'd just gotten from Richard.

"What a shock...on both counts," exclaimed Judy. "Wow. Your mom...Gosh.... And what a coward. I mean, really. An email?"

Robin admitted it was a hateful way to break the news. Now what should she do? Alone again, rejected and abandoned. Feeling empty. Starting all over. Does she jump on dating sites? Let friends know? It all seemed dismal and depressing. At 45, she didn't want to be out there marketing herself.

"Guys want those young things," she complained. "Or they want other guys..." she forced a laugh. The prospect of searching for a new relationship made her want to retch. "No one wants an old straight has-been."

"Just stop," Judy interrupted. "Change how you look at it. This is your time to work on you. Be the best version of you, from your heart."

"Is that what you do?" As soon as the words jumped out of her mouth, Robin wished she could recall them.

Judy took no offense. Instead she lectured Robin about how it's important to create a relationship with herself first and foremost. She needed to fill her own cup. "A lonely person looks for someone to fill them up, to love them. But when there are two empty people seeking to be filled up, neither has enough to give the other. It doesn't work." Judy paused to poignantly ask, "If you were looking for a relationship would you want to be in a relationship with you?"

Robin laughed uncomfortably, then stared down at her shoes, like a bad little girl in front of a parent who was scolding her. She knew Judy was serious. The concept was painful. Robin urged herself to be strong.

"Be someone you'd want to be with. Start by loving yourself," Judy pressed the point home.

"Jeeez, Jude. I feel like you just shot my brain with Novocain." She volleyed back, "Do you love you?"

"Ha. Good question. I didn't say it's easy. I work on it all the time. Some days are better than others. I struggle with relationships so I'm working on me"

Robin was taken aback by Judy's honesty, her vulnerability. It was a challenge for Robin to reveal any weakness. She hid emotions behind a carefree, adventurous exterior. Emotions to her were like nuts to a squirrel; she couldn't remember where she'd stored them. She feared if she faced the internal pain it would destroy her. She couldn't look too deeply inside. She couldn't let out the "real" Robin; she had to keep things buried, or so she believed.

"Look, I know you're wrestling with all that's happened. I think the Miami workshop is going to be good for you. It's about finding your power, not from a place of strength but from a place of yielding to who you truly are. Until we go, you should start keeping a journal. You're such a good writer and it might help to reveal to yourself how you feel and what you're experiencing."

Robin realized how afraid she was to give attention to her feelings. Putting personal thoughts on paper was scarier than facing the gang of Hells Angels who chased her once when she was not-so-surreptitiously photographing them for one of her articles. She'd learned so well how to avoid feeling. She'd just react to situations based on what she thought was expected, not from any authentic emotion that she'd allow to emerge.

As she listened to Judy, she realized how worthless she felt and how much she had numbed herself after losing her mother, her sister, her marriage, her true sense of who she was. Fear had become like a massive black cloak that formed boundaries and limitations.

"Forget a dating site, maybe I need a 'lost in the cosmos' site. Or a lobotomy. Yikes."

Judy suggested that Robin reach out to David, Robin's former massage therapist, and let him take her to his special spiritual reader. Robin protested that she hadn't talked to David in a couple of years. David had made overtures that were uncomfortable, so she stopped going to him. He was a nice enough guy, but Robin wasn't interested. And now why would she go to a "spiritual reader"?

Judy admitted that she'd run into David last week. "He came by the store to try one of my massage blends. He asked about you and instantly suggested he take you to Hannah, his reader," said Judy. "It couldn't hurt."

As timing would have it, Robin's phone began to buzz. "Let me call you back, Jude. It's David calling." They both laughed as Robin answered, "Hello stranger." After a pause, she added, "Judy was just telling me she ran into you and now here you are."

David prepared Robin for the session with Hannah, who was 82 with a serious heart problem. He warned that she was odd, quite flakey, but seriously gifted and extremely capable.

David and Robin drove in his 10-year-old silver Lexus to the flea market in Fort Myers, the town just north of Naples. They parked and David grabbed her hand to guide her through the dirty, run-down, tangled aisles of second-hand merchandise, worn-out home appliances, booths of decorative home accessories, cheap jewelry, and then, in the midst of it all was the shabby, green brocade curtain in a back corner.

"I won't go in with you," David said, his sandy hair falling around an appealingly handsome face. His soft brown eyes were kind and comforting. He was slim and fit, athletically packaged in his 5'9" stature. "Hannah is expecting you."

Robin already felt off-put by the surroundings and the hideous curtains, but she trusted David. For whatever reason, she felt divine intervention and needed this reading. She drew in a deep breath and parted the tattered drapes.

The tiny space was stuffy with barely room for the rickety table flanked by two chairs. No wonder David wouldn't join her. He would never have fit. Hannah was old, gray-skinned and sickly. She beckoned for Robin to sit in the empty chair across from her. She had short-cropped, thinning white hair and her face looked more wrinkled than a Sharpe puppy. But her glassy brown eyes had a purity and intelligence as she immediately took both Robin's hands in hers.

Under the flimsy card table, Hannah's skinny legs found Robin's and she wrapped herself like a pretzel around Robin's lower extremities. For a frail woman, Hannah had leg strength like an orangutan holding its offspring from slipping off a tree limb hanging precariously over a cliff. Robin was surprised as the moment felt awkward and yet strangely normal. Hannah was likeable and seemed to feed off Robin's energy. Hannah looked right through Robin's eyes as if connecting directly to her soul. It was unnerving but not frightening.

"You have no idea how powerful you are, do you?," she announced in a sweet, motherly voice. Robin just shrugged, having absolutely no idea where this conversation was going. Was this the reading? Staring into my eyes and feeling my energies? As if sensing her thoughts, Hannah announced she had important words for her and to listen carefully. Robin wondered if she was so transparent that her thoughts and feelings were hanging out there for anyone to see, like soap bubbles pouring out in disordered speckles of light. It was worrying that Judy, like her mother, had been able to see effortlessly beyond her thick emotional walls. And now Hannah.

"Don't be concerned. You are not an open book, little one."

The words hung in the air as if they had come directly from her own mother's lips. "You have much to give the world," said Hannah, tightening her grip on Robin's legs even more. Robin concentrated on keeping circulation moving through her lower limbs so they wouldn't turn numb. "You're a communicator and you need to open up your heart and your intuitive awareness. You will be meeting someone who will help you."

She smiled knowingly at Robin, but Robin wasn't sure about the meaning behind her expression. Hannah looked amused and satisfied. Robin was dying to know exactly what Hannah was thinking but didn't want to interrupt.

"I see a very attractive man coming towards you." Robin immediately flashed on the handsome image of Richard and just as quickly dismissed the thought of him coming back into her life. After all, he was in Paris… with another man. Crap.

"You haven't met him yet. But the time is coming. Life is a tapestry of experiences. Enjoy every moment. Be in joy. Know the vitality of being. You have much to share. That's it."

What's it? thought Robin. "Can I ask a question?," she managed weakly.

Hannah's aged face slowly nodded.

"Do you know what happened to my mother? Can you see her?"

Hannah closed her eyes and began breathing erratically. Robin felt a hot flash of concern pulse up her spine that something awful was taking place in Hannah's ill body right before her eyes. What would I do if she had a heart attack in front of me? Then Hannah convulsed and began speaking in a different voice.

"Just be content to know that I'm okay. I'm always with you and Jean. You two have work to do. I will always love you, little one."

Robin was startled and shaken. It was her mother's voice. How could that be?

And with that, Hannah abruptly disengaged her legs and released Robin's hands. Their connection ended along with the session. In a thin puzzled voice, Robin thanked Hannah and pushed through the ugly curtains to find David waiting for her on the other side.

"How was it?," David asked.

"Strange."

"I know. But just let it all sink in."

"I will try." Robin felt drained, her legs wobbling with each step. David took her hand to steady her out of the maze.

"I'm having some special friends over tonight for a cookout. Why don't you come? Say seven?

Robin didn't feel very social. Her inclination was to decline.

"You may remember me telling you about my buddy Adam Anderson, the musician? He's now using a unique technique for healing clients with music. Might be interesting for the article Judy told me you're working on."

She wanted to decline, return home and soak alone with her thoughts in a warm bath.

But she was intrigued and didn't want to blow off an opportunity to learn more about sound therapies.

"Sounds interesting. Thanks, David. Sure."

Like mother, like daughter. Robin had an insatiable curiosity and couldn't pass up the possibility of a good story. Further, she rationalized she had to get out more, meet new people, expand her social circles. Meet someone new. Maybe Hannah's prediction would be realized tonight!

But hours later, when the time came to get ready, she regretted that she'd accepted the invitation. She was lethargic and didn't want to have to be "on," making small talk and acting charming. She especially did not want to encourage David's attention, at least not in the way in which he always seemed interested. But then again, David had said these were "special" friends so maybe it wouldn't be the usual gathering of superficial people looking for a sexual encounter. Maybe it would be something more dynamic. And Adam did sound interesting. Besides, she was getting hungry and all she had in her refrigerator were a half-carton of almond milk and a half-eaten apple. One of David's creative cookouts would be nourishing.

Moving at a snail's pace, she put on white jeans and an oversized collared pink shirt, adding exotic dangling silver earrings and casual white sandals. Dabbing on a little peach blush on her tanned cheeks and adding a hint of lipstick, she assessed herself in the mirror through her subtle, tired-looking brown eyes. Her soft, straight honey-brown hair cascaded gently on her shoulders. It'll have to do.

She decided to stop at her favorite bakery to pick up a sinful dessert for the party. She believed in the law of reciprocity and wanted to contribute to the gathering with the small gesture of a treat. She knew David would appreciate the effort and she owed him.

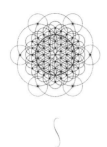

CHAPTER ELEVEN

*D*avid lived in a large home on a corner lot in North Naples with a graciously landscaped yard overlooking a quiet lake and an oversized lanai occupied on one end by a lap pool and hot tub. The opposite end had a full outdoor kitchen. The house had a separate entrance that delivered clients directly into his massage studio space, although with certain clients he'd use the grand lanai giving that outdoor, be-in-nature experience which was always well-received.

Tonight, the lanai was set with two contiguous tables draped in orange and yellow floral tablecloths for a buffet-style dinner. Drinks were arranged near the pool area. When Robin arrived, David was busy working at the grill while several of the half-dozen guests were hanging out with him as they sipped on drinks with their glasses sweating in the humidity.

With an emphasis on health, David was whipping up free-range chicken and shrimp kabobs with pineapple, tomatoes and green peppers. It looked like a colorful meal out of the entertainment pages of a trendy lifestyle magazine.

"Smells delicious," Robin said loudly as she approached the group around David. "I brought these for dessert. They're mini gluten-free Bundt cakes."

David turned and smiled, gave her a light hug, and made introductions. Cynthia was a skinny brunette with a childlike laugh. Adam was the musician he'd mentioned earlier. Peter, who hadn't missed too many beers judging from the roundness of his belly, was visiting from Sydney, Australia and had the charming accent to go with his birthplace. David thanked Robin for the adorable bundtinis and put them in the mini refrigerator.

Over by the drinks were Rhonda and James, the only married couple at the gathering, who were talking to Melanie, a realtor who looked cool and comfortable in a loose white sundress. Melanie had an effusive, bubbly personality and thick blonde curls that seemed in kinetic motion dancing with each dramatic gesture as she talked incessantly. She had already sniffed out a possibility that the couple was hunting for a new home. She had them cornered with her sassy gift of gab and frankly, they seemed to not mind listening to the animated doll face.

The grill made sizzling noises. Cynthia commented that David was a master at making dinners that tasted amazing and had the additional benefit of being nutritious. She rambled that because of his massage therapy, he was genuinely concerned about feeding the body properly. She was sounding like his public relations agent but perhaps she was just enamored with him and was scoring some well-placed brownie points. She continued to ingratiate herself.

Adam offered Robin a drink and strutted back with a glass of red wine at her request, leaning down to deliver it. Adam was basketball-player height at 6'5" and had shoulder-length black and silvery tight curls that framed a narrow, chiseled tanned face which contrasted with his green, spirited eyes. He wore a choker of blue-green turquoise over a black fitted tee shirt and black jeans. The colors made his eyes sparkle brightly. Robin guessed he was in his early fifties. He was eager to talk about his work and wasted little time in keeping Robin's attention. He had a rich captivating voice that could have played well on radio.

He'd been performing music since he was six years old growing up in an artistic family in Cleveland. His mother was a singer and his dad played accordion when he wasn't doing long hauls as a trucker. Adam started on piano but quickly took up the guitar and became addicted to both acoustic and electric, performing in neighborhood bands and serving as the lead singer in many of them. The passion for music shone in his eyes.

"There's nothing like the vibrational impact of a guitar against your body as you play," he swooned. "It's orgasmic." He laughed heartily and Robin was drawn into his joyfulness.

"Music isn't just an experience for your ears. It isn't just sounds. Every cell in your body feels the vibrations and responds. It's about energy and frequencies. It's so much more powerful than people realize," he said.

Robin was stimulated by the conversation, soaking up the deep, resonant sounds of Adam's voice and the meaning of his words. Her impression of a typical musician shattered before her very eyes like glass hit by a single bullet disintegrating into shiny slivers. Adam wasn't just rhythm and flash. He was probing and philosophical. She liked his curiosity and experimentation.

They sat separated from the others on cushioned rattan and wrought-iron chairs set on the far side of the lanai. Adam easily pulled the heavy outdoor chair closer to Robin. A cool breeze whispering off the lake gently brushed their faces. Adam worked full-time as a musician, playing gigs around town which were mostly evenings and weekends. In between, he was researching and practicing a new kind of therapeutic music which Robin was curious to know more about.

"David told me you're actually using sounds with clients who are suffering various ailments. Please do tell."

Suddenly a loud cowbell jangled through the peacefulness of the lanai and all eyes turned towards the disturbance.

"Time to eat," announced David, as he gleefully held high the noisemaking cowbell. It tickled him to impact people in different ways and now he was amused by everyone's startled reactions.

Laid out on the floral tablecloths was a sumptuous buffet. "Start at this end," David instructed, pointing to the plates and silverware. The couple who had been captured in conversation by the neighborhood realtor were first in line, an excuse to detach from the claws of a salesperson. Finally, they'd had their fill of her pitches for the best communities they should consider. Now solo, the realtor, Melanie, sauntered toward the oversized rattan chairs, introducing herself again to Robin and reaching up to give Adam a hug.

"How are you, big boy? How's the music biz?"

"Doing well, thanks. Haven't seen you at any of the local hangouts lately."

"My daughter's come home to roost. She was terminated from her job in Chicago. She's been licking her wounds and I've been applying the salve."

"How motherly of you," said Adam in an almost mocking tone. His body language clearly indicated disapproval of Melanie, her style, her ideas. But Robin sensed he tried to reel in his attitude with a more caring question.

"What kind of work does she do?"

"She was assistant manager of an indoor mall off the Magnificent Mile on Michigan Avenue. She didn't think it was so magnificent when they downsized and booted her out."

"Did she like living in Chicago?," Robin chimed in.

"We used to live in the suburbs there. So, yeah. She has lots of friends in the city. But now she's here. I'm trying to get her into my business, but she has no interest. So, we'll see…." Her facial expression dropped into a forlorn look. "She probably won't stay here much longer."

The buffet line beckoned and Adam gallantly motioned for the two women to go ahead of him. Melanie was now between Robin and Adam making Robin feel robbed of her conversation. Perhaps they had been antisocial by keeping to themselves.

Cynthia began flitting about as if she were the hostess of the evening, approaching each guest to find out if they needed a drink replenishment. Robin could hear the clinking of ice cubes and slosh of liquids as Melanie and Adam behind her shook their glasses. Robin raised her half-filled red wine up in the air. No, everyone seemed quite content.

David, in his khaki shorts, flip-flops and tight yellow tee shirt, stood by the grill and beamed over the seeming success of the gathering. Entertaining was a natural for him; he did it effortlessly and obviously enjoyed every minute. Smug satisfaction showed in his expression. Then he strolled over to Robin, putting his arm around her shoulders, and whispered into her ear, his clean-shaven face almost touching hers. The scent of his musky cologne wafted into her nostrils.

"You doing okay?"

"Absolutely. This is amazing what you've put together. Thanks, David. Really!" She pecked his cheek in what she felt was an obligatory show of approval.

"Lookin' good," he nodded at Robin knowingly, gesturing with a thumbs up. "Smooth operator."

Robin wasn't quite sure what David was intimating but she didn't want to create any waves that she couldn't swim through at the moment. She'd had a full day already with Hannah's strange session. She just smiled as a punctuated end to the subtle interaction.

"What a dinna," exclaimed Peter in his Aussie slang. "I'll need another frostie to wash down all this grub," he called to Cynthia.

"Coming right up," she acknowledged.

The remainder of the evening was uneventful. David and Peter seemed to be holding court for Melanie and Cynthia in one part of the outdoor setting. Adam and Robin chatted with Rhonda and James, who it turned out had absolutely no inclination to buy a new home in town but admitted they were being polite.

As Robin finished her second glass of wine, she enjoyed the praises she got for bringing the bundtinis for a sweet finale. The evening was winding down and so was Robin. It was time to depart so she began to say her goodbyes at which point Adam quickly suggested continuing their earlier conversation over lunch. Robin admitted she'd like that but had a full schedule the next day. They settled on the day after and would meet at the outdoor bar area on the patio at Brio's at "high noon," suggested Adam. "Now you're sounding like a gunslinger," quipped Robin in agreement.

~

Knowing a Friday lunch hour at such a popular North Naples restaurant would be busy, Adam arrived early to secure a table with a good view of the front so he wouldn't miss Robin's entrance. He liked her walk, a straight, no-nonsense gait that gave her an appealing air of confidence. Some might perceive her body language as arrogance, but many people found her movements attractive.

Adam wore his self-imposed black uniform, a tee shirt, jeans, and boots, his long curly hair tied back in a ponytail. He'd performed the previous night at a local sports pub and then jammed with musician friends until the wee hours of the morning so he was weary, a little hungover but excited to be seeing Robin again and sharing his work with her.

It was a breezy day in mid-June with temperatures rising into the high eighties, signaling that the hot summer months were approaching. But the humidity level was thankfully low, keeping the air fresh and comfortable on this glorious day. Birds were chirping wildly, and the restaurant was already abuzz with activity.

Adam seemed lost in a daydream. Suddenly Robin's voice cut through his reverie and he jumped slightly.

"You snuck up on me." He smiled, standing to greet Robin.

"Just call me Ninja. Although you're the one with the look." Robin stepped back and waved her hand as if presenting Adam's outfit as evidence.

Robin wore a casual, strapless pink and white polka dot sundress with long white feathered earrings and, in deference to Adam's height, white sandals with two-inch heels, which didn't have much of an impact in altering their significant height difference.

Adam towered at least a head taller. He gave her a quick hug and pulled out the chair gesturing to Robin. "Please."

"Thanks." Robin was holding her hem, so the breeze didn't reveal more than she wanted as she sidled onto the chair.

"Red wine?"

"Yes. Thank you for remembering. Cabernet would be lovely."

A young man with close set eyes, jet black hair and dark skin stopped at the table to introduce himself as Julio, their server, and to take a drink order. He asked if they had any questions about the menu and when they didn't, he headed off to the bar. He was slight of stature and walked as if the heels of his shoes were made of coiled springs that never quite touched the ground.

"So that was a great barbecue. David's a gifted host," Adam stated.

Robin agreed, feeling captivated by Adam's deep green eyes. He had an interesting appearance that had a whimsical edge. They chatted about some of David's guests.

"And that Melanie…" Adam began.

Robin looked away. She knew it was human nature to talk about someone like Melanie who was such a caricature of a person. Yet she didn't want to judge or gossip. It wasn't a good topic she wished to pursue. Fortunately, they were quickly interrupted as Julio returned, setting a giant wide-mouthed wine goblet in front of Robin. The large, rounded glass dwarfed the amount of red liquid that it contained, much to Robin's relief. Normally she didn't drink during the day at all…that is, unless she was in the South of France.

For a fleeting moment, it all felt reminiscent of Arles, the outdoor setting, the warm wisps of air, the golden sunlight and intense Mediterranean colors of blues, greens, warm terracotta, lavenders, and yellows. She brought herself back to the present in time to toast her glass against Adam's manly bottle of dark beer.

"To music," he said with a full smile showing off gleaming white teeth like a perfect string of pearls. Robin mused about performers and how keen appearances had to be. She wondered if his million-dollar smile was expensive. He was certainly well put together and obviously vested in how he presented himself. For someone his height, he had excellent posture and owned his physical attributes, but Robin sensed he had a streak of narcissism or perhaps it was just his ego showing. After all, he was a showman and needed that strong sense of self to get up on stage in front of judgmental eyes and ears critiquing his every move.

"To beautiful sounds," Robin countered, finally damming the flood of thoughts to stop their flow.

Julio came springing back in a blur of action to take their order. Robin asked for the chopped salad with shrimp, vinaigrette dressing on the side. Adam requested the pesto chicken club sandwich and another beer. Robin was still nursing her wine gingerly. She had skipped breakfast and didn't want too much alcohol on an empty stomach in front of someone she hardly knew. She wanted to keep her wits about her and be clear-headed to learn more about his experimental music.

"You'll have to taste my sandwich. It's one of the best dishes here."

The comment forced a smile to erupt across Robin's face as she remembered her mother's advice when she was still a teenager that a girl should spend time with the boys who want to share their lunch with you and not with the ones who want to take yours.

"Tell me about your work."

"I've always been fascinated by the way music affects people." Adam took a slug of his beer to finish it before the new bottle was delivered. "Back in Ohio, my mother met this woman who started a music program in Cleveland at University Hospitals where my mom worked. This woman, Laney, performed miracles at the bedsides of sick and dying people. I was a teenager playing music around town in bands and my mother would come home from work and talk about the amazing benefits this woman doctor was having on patients by singing, playing instruments or composing music. Extremely sick people would relax, become less anxious, feel less pain, and improve. I was inspired by the stories my mother shared. Then later when I was at college in Boston, I met another woman who was doing research at Mass General quantifying how music therapy can improve medical outcomes. I got hooked."

"So, you became a music therapist?"

"Not exactly. Probably should have. I'm a renegade. March to the beat of a different drummer as they say."

"I can relate," Robin smiled encouragingly. "I've always been a bit out there myself."

"I started doing my own experimentation, mostly to help friends. My friend Eric got bladder cancer, Jeff had surgery for a slipped disk and Barbara had lymphoma. I began composing special music and playing my guitar for them. I'd observe and document reactions and progress. As I noticed certain notes that helped their condition improve, I made audio recordings so they could continue to use my sounds as part of their therapy. It was immensely rewarding. You can just imagine. For so many years I was criticized by friends as having no ambition, being a lowly musician. But then suddenly, my lowly profession was helping them recover. I went deeper and studied the energy of music and things like Solfeggio frequencies. In fact, Solfeggio tones were used way back in ancient times. They were fundamental in both Western Christianity and Eastern Indian religions in Gregorian and Sanskrit chants." He paused to make eye contact and check if Robin was glazing over or genuinely interested.

"Go on," Robin prompted, wanting to know more. She hung on every word and wished she'd brought her recorder. Her phone would only handle a few minutes of audio and she wanted to capture every word. She rummaged in her purse and pulled out a small notepad and pen.

"Do you mind if I make some notes?" She chortled at her inadvertent pun as she spread her writing pad on the placemat in front of her.

"Sure."

Julio bounded back to the table to deliver their lunches. Robin had to clear the way, picking up her pad and holding it tightly against her body as Julio, with artistic flourish, laid an oversized decorative bowl with her salad on the table in front of her and put a lovely ceramic filled with dressing next to it. He then placed an enormous, bigger-than-mouth-sized sandwich in front of Adam.

"Thank you, Julio." He turned to Robin. "See, you must have a taste. It's huge," he said, emphasizing the last word as he cut a generous section of the sandwich, holding it airborne between his knife and fork not knowing where to put it. Finally, he delicately placed it on top of her salad.

"Thanks. Looks amazing."

Robin was fascinated. This tall, green-eyed, long-haired musician had more depth than she would have assumed by his appearance. He treated people with respect. He had passion and curiosity. Personal discoveries were fueling his enthusiasm. It was fun to listen and she suddenly felt privileged to know about his findings. "Never judge a book by its cover," popped into her mind, which was such an old cliché but ever more relevant in this situation.

Suddenly crashing through the flow of conversation, Robin's phone buzzed wildly. The ringer was off, but the vibration was enough to make her jump. She glanced down at the screen to see Nan's name and a picture of her smiling face. Oddly, she felt sucker punched. A sense of foreboding sent a chill down her spine. She decided to respond with a text that she'd call her back.

"Everything okay?" Adam's expression showed concern at the flicker of disturbance in Robin's coppery eyes.

"I'm sure all is well…" Robin countered, trying to sound secure in her answer but harboring a hint of doubt. Still, she didn't want to interrupt their discussion. "I'll call her after lunch."

Adam re-started his commentary about Solfeggio tones when the phone buzzed again, this time with a text.

"Sorry." Robin broke eye contact with Adam and looked down again at her screen. Another icy ripple coursed through her body as she read Nan's text: Urgent, PLEASE. Call as soon as you can.

Robin tried to neutralize her growing panic. Nervous pulsations were oozing down her arms and legs like an oil spill. It was unlike Nan to send such a message but still she felt that whatever it was could wait until after lunch. Again, she apologized to Adam and urged him to continue.

"Do you need to call someone?"

"Eventually. I'll deal with it. Can't be life or death." As she said the words, she wondered if she was making a bad choice. She desperately wanted to be present in this moment and finish her lunch with Adam. Determination won but the impending call to Nan hung over her like a spreading fog descending to obliterate the mountaintop of her mind. She was finding it hard to concentrate.

"Please continue." Robin forced her eyes to focus on Adam while her heart threatened to distract her with loud thumping. Her appetite had vanished. She played with bits of salad on her fork.

"I'm sure you've already discovered from your research that every human cell responds to frequency and vibration. Solfeggio frequencies have specific tones that interact in healthy ways and affect the conscious and subconscious mind and the physical body." He paused to squash down his sandwich enough so he could take a bite. He chewed in silence, took a slug of beer and regathered his thoughts.

"Can you send me links to details?" Robin had put down her fork to make scribbles on her pad.

"Absolutely. In fact, the research in modern times by genetic biochemists have revealed healing frequencies that can repair damaged DNA. I can send you that information. Are you familiar with the Schumann Resonance?"

"Not really. What does that have to do with any of this?"

"So, earth has a heartbeat. There are electromagnetic waves, discovered by Schumann, that exist between the earth's surface and the ionosphere. The Solfeggio tones resonate in harmony with these frequencies. Our bodies are influenced by all of this much more than we consciously realize."

"In fact," he continued, "the advent of rubber soled shoes began to block us from feeling the planet's energies. People started getting out of balance and suffered anxiety, depression and diseases. Living in jammed high-rise steel cities is also unhealthy. That's why walking barefoot on the beach is so uplifting. You're bringing your body and mind into alignment with the natural rhythms of nature. In my music, I consciously incorporate these tones for different purposes."

"How do you mean?" Robin tipped up her wine glass to finish the last drop. Her food sat before her still barely touched. Her stomach was doing flip flops and she could feel the warmth of the alcohol slightly fogging her brain. She wanted to stay engaged in the conversation but her mind kept wandering. What was Nan's urgency?

"For instance, when working with people with diagnosed illnesses, I mostly use 528 HZ for its reparative effects. It's miraculously healing and energizing. Been shown to repair our biological building blocks at the cellular level."

"Remarkable." Robin interjected dully. She needed to make the call. She should not have procrastinated and was becoming impatient to reach Nan. She needed to know what was wrong.

"Ancient musical instruments were tuned to 432 Hz which resonates with the Schumann frequency and has a soothing effect. It's often incorporated in yoga and meditation music because it fills the mind with feelings of peace and well-being. It resonates perfectly with our brain waves." He paused, evaluating Robin's vacant stare. "Looks like right about now you could use its calming effects. Are you okay?"

She wiped her mouth with her napkin and shook her head, attempting to clear her mind.

"Adam, I'm so sorry. I need to go. Can we get the waiter to box up my meal?"

She mindlessly dropped her pen and pad back into her purse and pulled out her wallet.

"Sure." He reached out to touch her hand holding a credit card. "Put that away. I'll take care of this."

She was feeling too distraught to argue. Lunch ended with an anticlimactic thud, a hug, and Robin rushed off to her car to make the call to Nan. Adam shrugged as he watched her go. She was struggling to balance her purse and the take-out bag while searching for her keys.

Throwing all her stuff on the passenger seat, she started the car, turned on the AC and grabbed her phone, hitting the call button for Nan.

"Oh Robin," Nan's voice sounded strained and tense. "It's your decision but I'd recommend you get on a plane and come to New York right away."

"Why? Wh-what's going on?"

"There's no sugar-coating it. Your sister is in the hospital. The doctors label it an IDO. An intentional drug overdose. George says it's serious. They had to intubate. You know, put a tube in her airway to keep her breathing. You should be here as soon as you can get a flight."

Robin's mind spun thinking of Jean lying in a hospital bed. Her shoulders became tight and pressed up towards her ears, so it made her neck disappear. Her heart hurt for her sister. She regretted their estrangement, and it made her question whether her presence would be helpful or harmful.

"OMG. How awful. Is her husband with her?"

Nan's breathing became audibly labored as if she were having an allergic reaction to the question. After an uncomfortable pause, she finally admitted, "The truth is, he left her."

"No way! What happened?"

"They separated a few weeks ago. No one knew. Nathan just moved out. Gone. Abandoned her. We don't even know how to reach him. I knew she was having issues. I told you I had connected her with a psychiatrist. Robin, you're her only family. Can you come?"

"Let me see if I can find a flight out tonight."

"If you fly into JFK, I can pick you up. She's at Long Island Community Hospital. You can stay with me and George until things settle. Or I'm happy to find a hotel near the hospital and stay with you."

"I'll call you when I figure it all out."

"Love you," said Nan in a reassuring tone.

In the blink of an eye, life changed. Plans changed. From a fascinating lunch with an interesting man, Robin's attention was now fully on her sister, their past and this moment of trauma. Robin could not escape the irony that Jean lived in Amityville, a small diverse coastal village that yielded *The Amityville Horror*. Poor Jean was now living her own version of horror and Robin would become a player in this movie.

She had a choice. She could choose not to go, not to support her sister in her moment of trauma, not to be by her side. She could dismiss any responsibility or accountability and go for a walk on the beach. Go back to working on her assignments. Be in her happy condo. Ignore this truth. After all, Jean made it painfully clear that she hated Robin.

But maybe, just maybe she could change that.

Still rooted in the driver's seat of her parked car with the AC blasting, she took a full breath and let it out with a cleansing sigh. She looked deeply inside herself. She could just say no. But she couldn't. She caressed the locket that, since Arles, always hung around her neck, with two loving sisters pictured inside together. Robin couldn't live with herself if she just stayed detached, unwilling to lift a finger. Her sister could die. Robin wasn't that kind of person. Her mother wasn't that kind of person and, if Ruth were watching, she'd be furious. She owed it to her family. She and her sister were all that remained of the Stevens clan. I cannot let Jean go through this alone. I must go.

Balancing her phone in her lap, she searched for flights. Fort Myers to John F. Kennedy International Airport, New York City. A flight was leaving that evening at 6:46, arriving at 9:25. It was now just a few minutes after one. She could make it happen. She could be on that flight. Did she want to go? No. But would she? Yes. She booked the flight, a first step in making good on her promise to herself to make amends with Jean.

Shifting the car into drive, she had to get home and pack. She began thinking about all that she needed to do and what she needed to take. As she drove, she auto-dialed Judy who answered on the second ring.

"Any chance you could drive me to the airport at 5:15 this afternoon? I have to go to New York." She was proud of herself that she was able to maintain a stable, unrevealing voice. Then she remembered who she was talking to.

"Obviously, something's wrong. Yes. I can take you. What's up? Talk to me."

Besides having a keen sixth sense, Judy was one of those true friends who was always ready to do what needed to be done. She gave Robin's life a richness and fullness. Robin hoped that she was as good a friend to Judy. She quickly explained the news about Jean and asked if she could brew up one of her mysterious alchemies of aromatherapy that

Robin could bring to help her sister. Judy would be at Robin's condo at 5 p.m. to allow extra time in case of traffic and said she had the perfect blend for Jean. In parting, she reminded Robin that they had to be in Miami next week for Uriel's workshop.

"I haven't forgotten. Nice that you're on a first name basis," Robin kidded. "I'll be back in time." Under her breath, she hoped that was true and decided she would make it true. She owed it to herself to get to the workshop. She'd do absolutely everything she could do for her sister and then she'd be back.

Once home, she was a speed demon, a blur of action trying in a mad dash to get ready in just hours. A load of laundry was essential, so she'd have clean underwear. Having been domestically negligent, she was now paying for her avoidance. She organized her toiletries into one compartment of her suitcase. She needed to take enough of her research papers to set up interviews and maybe even write some of the article while she was away. These were tucked into another pocket of her carry-on. And then clothes. What to take? In Naples, she wore bright parrot-like colors, but New York required a completely different palette. She frantically ransacked the closet. The surface of her bed was rapidly strewn with dark options of blacks, browns and beiges, skirts, slacks, shirts, a pair of shorts, sneakers, heels, boots. Where's my light jacket? It can get cool. The room resembled the aftermath of a small tornado. Think. What else do I need? Take a break.

She padded to the kitchen for a strong cup of coffee. Pausing to sit by the window, she sipped the hot liquid and gazed out at her neighborhood lake. Lacy, elegant palm trees in varying tones of greens surrounded the blue waters in stillness, which reflected blue skies and puffy white clouds. Blooming flower gardens dotted the outside of buildings on the opposite shore. There was a quiet emptiness, except for one lone anhinga perched at the edge of the lake, wings spread, neck stretched, beak pointed. White feathers on its shoulders were much like the ones that dangled from Robin's ears. Yes…pack earrings.

She wondered if the bird felt lonely by itself, with no other apparent creatures in the vicinity for company. Her mind turned to thoughts of her sister and the loneliness she must have felt to descend into such an emotional abyss. Suicide. How does someone reach that level of despair and hopelessness? Thoughts welled up of her husband and his threats. Whew. Her anger towards her sister for the many years of rejections was melting into a dull sadness. It seemed obvious that there was much she didn't know about her sister's life, a person she'd known since birth who emerged from the same gene pool separated by a few scant years. What was it going to be like to see Jean now in her terrible state of mind? Robin felt afraid. She pushed down the fear that was rising in her throat. How would my sister react to me? Am I strong enough to deal with her? Am I ready to face this ordeal?

In the other room, her phone played the "Nan" ringtone, which pulled her back from the riddle of questions. She ran to answer. "Hello Nan! Everything okay?"

"Yes. So far. Since I know you never have bags, I'll pick you up at arrivals. Also, my husband suggested we stay at a hotel. My home is about a 90-minute drive and we're going to want to be closer. I reserved a double for us."

"Thanks, Nan. See you at 9:25."

Robin went back to packing. She was grateful that Nan would be with her. It would help her feel better equipped and she'd have someone who could help her not to overreact. She was going with the hope that she could reclaim a sister, rekindle their sisterhood. She was feeling buzzy from the java as she swiftly finished packing.

Judy was prompt in picking her up, bounding through the front door in a lime green halter top and brown speckled yoga pants shouting, "Your chauffeur has arrived." As Robin vaulted down the stairs with her stuffed carry-on bag over one shoulder and her purse over the other, she chuckled at Judy. "You look like a damn tree that should be growing in my yard."

"Just call me cab," said Judy. "For cabbage palm and taxi. A combo, at your service." She inclined her head bowing with a flourish as if taking a final curtain call, inadvertently dislodging her long blonde hair from the unkempt bun she'd fastened to the top of her head. "Oops," she grabbed at the mass of locks covering her face and re-organized the messy tangle back into a clip, then reached out a hand. "May I take something?"

"Nah. I'm good. I can handle this." Robin waggled her bags. "This is the easy part. Frankly, I'm just not sure I can handle my sister and...." She paused as she loaded her stuff and herself into the car.

"...all that baggage. This could make us or break us forever."

The comment hung in the air like a festering wound. Once on the way to the airport, Judy offered salve in the form of advice.

"You've made the right decision to go. So, change the way you look at the whole thing. Instead of seeing it as a breaking point, something awful, see it as a breakthrough point. This is an opening to reconcile with your sister, to help her through her pain and in the process to release your pain."

"My pain?" Robin sounded insulted.

"You know what I'm saying."

Robin had held onto the rift with Jean for so long that anytime she'd think of her sister, she'd habitually default to a reaction of dismissal, even disappointment. She had no expectation of ever soliciting caring, kindness or love from her sister. Those emotions weren't there. Had they ever been there? Now those feelings seemed even less attainable, especially now after all the years. This hole had been punctured through her heart so long ago that she had gotten comfortable with it as merely another tragic loss. If it healed, closed, what would replace the dark emptiness? She knew how to battle with the agony of hurt, she wasn't sure she understood how to accept anything else.

"Yeah, I know," Robin admitted after an exceedingly long pause. "It's tough."

"Only if you allow it to be tough. You can choose to make it easier. Oh, before I forget, here's a blend for your sister, and one for you." Judy pulled two thin vials out of her pocket. "Yours has the pink label."

Robin tossed the tiny bottles into her purse without even looking at them. Her mind was on other things and her nerves were jagged. "You'd benefit from using yours right now." Robin listened absently, not really registering a single word. She was staring out the window, filled with trepidation.

"Robin!" Judy was loud enough to draw her attention. "Please use your blend right now. It will help calm those swirling thoughts that I can see are sending you into orbit, and not in a good way."

Robin dutifully obeyed like a child who's been chastised to take vitamins and drink her juice. She rummaged through her bag and retrieved the one marked in delicate pink letters that said, "Soothe Time." She examined the ingredients: lavender, chamomile, peppermint, and olive oil before sliding off the top to reveal a rollerball. Judy saw her hesitation. "Smell it to make sure you like it and roll it on your neck and inside your wrists."

Robin took a deep inhalation of the relaxing potion and exhaled with an exaggerated sigh which immediately broke the tension. They both laughed.

"That is soothing," Robin confessed once the giggles subsided and she finished rolling it on her body. "Thanks, Judy."

"You've got this!," Judy exclaimed.

Robin wasn't so sure.

CHAPTER TWELVE

*R*obin rolled her carry-on suitcase out the arrivals door at JFK into the brisk evening air. Her nostrils smacked instantly with diesel fumes. The platform was filled with a cacophony of sounds and blurs of light and movement. Car horns blared, buses, taxis, and cars jockeyed for position along the curb, and people hurriedly buzzed past her. She could sense her body withdrawing into the city mode of self-preservation. No eye contact. No interaction. Keep my posture strong, body tight. Avoid becoming a sloppy victim. Walk with determination. But she wasn't sure where she was going. She found a column to lean against so she could stop and call Nan without getting stampeded. It was 9:30.

"I'm here. Outside arrivals. What kind of car do you have?"

"Silver BMW. I was early and had to circle. I'm coming back through now. Be at the front of the platform. There's some construction. It's a mess. Hey, I'm glad you're here."

Robin piled herself into Nan's sporty car, dragging her luggage in as quickly as possible to avoid being run over by the unruly traffic. She blew an air kiss at Nan and settled into the passenger seat with a cathartic sigh. She breathed in the smell of new car leather.

"I'm so happy to see you," Nan gave Robin a quick glance. "You look good." Nan reached over and patted Robin's thigh in an affectionate gesture.

Robin had on a bright red zip-up turtleneck, a light, black leather jacket, blue jeans, and ankle-high black leather boots. Her honey brown hair cascaded loosely around her shoulders framing her tanned face.

"Thanks. So, do you. I like your hair like that."

Nan's ash-blonde hair was chin length, a bit shorter than usual. She wore a fashionable blue scarf over a black pullover, setting off her sapphire eyes and pale, pink skin, which was the color of an aging magnolia blossom. Wrinkle lines appeared deep with fatigue.

"I appreciate you alerting me about Jean."

"I visited her today."

"And…?"

"She looks bad, ragged. But not as bad as I expected. She's not on a ventilator. The hospital gave me misinformation."

"So that's good…not the misinformation but that she's not been intubated."

"Right. She's in a private room."

"So, what happened exactly?"

"Apparently she stopped seeing her psychiatrist but stock-piled her medication. She was prescribed clonazepam, a benzodiazepine that reduces anxiety and insomnia. Two weeks after Nathan unceremoniously left her, she started drinking heavily and intentionally took pills. Said there was no reason to be alive. No one cared. Thank God a neighbor stopped by to return a pot she'd borrowed and found her unconscious on her kitchen floor."

"Did you tell her I'm coming?"

"Yes."

"What'd she say?"

"Nothing. She isn't very conversant. She seems confused and her breathing is a bit slow. She doesn't look like herself."

Robin got quiet. It'd been so long since she'd seen her, she didn't even know what her sister would look like. She was caught between hating her sister for all the years of abuse and an overwhelming feeling of sorrow for her, for doing this to herself, for the emptiness of her existence. Robin fiddled with the zipper on her shirt, pulling it tighter around her neck. She wasn't cold but felt a chill of concern move through her body. She hoped she hadn't made a big mistake in coming to see Jean.

Nan cut through her busy thoughts. "I found a Hilton Garden about 15 minutes away in Stony Brook. Visiting hours tomorrow begin at one. You hungry?"

"Not really. Haven't been hungry since you called me with the news."

"I know. I know how hard this is for you."

Robin looked down at her hands, barely seeing them in the darkness of the car. "I don't know how to be with her. I-I'm nervous."

"Just be yourself. Be open. Trust that all will be okay. This experience could be the catalyst for your sister to finally let go of the past. And you, too."

"Maybe." Robin felt tired and weak. The stress of doing the right thing was taking a toll.

"How 'bout we get you settled in the hotel and have a glass of wine?"

"Sure." Robin eyed Nan as she focused on the road. Streams of lights, mostly luminous red taillights, gleamed through the windshield creating artistic patterns on Nan's serious face. The traffic was still heavy at almost 10. In a way, being with Nan felt like a continuation of their European trip just a few weeks earlier. Here they were driving to another giant leap into the past. Robin was suddenly flashing on Stephanie, missing her artsy-ness and her humor. She was also missing her own sense of curiosity and courage. She steeled herself as she thought about seeing Jean in the hospital after what she tried to do to herself.

It was early afternoon the next day when Nan and Robin headed to the hospital. The Long Island skies were a gloomy dull gray that threatened storms, seeming to reflect the inner agitation building like a tornado within Robin's belly. They stopped at a cute café on the University campus to have brunch, but Robin hardly touched her eggs and pancakes as her stomach ached almost as much as her heart. She was troubled by the unknown that was coming closer every minute, the unknown of how her sister would behave. The experience was nerve-wracking and stressful.

Nan and Robin arrived at the hospital before 1 p.m. The half-century-old institution was a typical brick-faced two-story building, lavishly modernized with massive glass windows. They entered the reception area of vanilla walls punctuated with a faux-wood circular reception desk beneath stark fluorescent lights. An elderly woman with perfectly coiffed short grey hair, a reddish round face and an affable personality greeted them and suggested they wait in the lounge until visiting hours officially began.

As the two women settled down in the waiting area, Robin searched her purse for the pretty, pink-labeled bottle that Judy had given her. She dabbed the fragrant liquid from the rollerball onto her wrists and onto her index finger, rubbing her finger under her nose. Nan watched her actions questioningly.

"Want some?" Robin offered the vial.

"What is it?"

"Special essential oils that Judy blended for me. It helps."

"Sure." Nan tentatively put some on her finger and inhaled. "Hmmm. That's really pleasant."

"It's very calming. She created one for me to give to Jean. A different blend. I don't know what it is"

Just then, a short, balding man in a lab coat stepped into the lounge and announced that visiting hours had started and asked if they knew what room they needed to find. Nan was in charge and already knew.

"Here we go," said Robin, not meaning to say the words aloud.

Nan patted her arm comfortingly.

Room 211 was on the second floor. Nan pushed open the large heavy door with Robin trailing slightly behind but close enough to see a part of a bed on the cold institutional tile floor. Fully inside, Robin was struck by the unpleasant smells of disinfectant mixed with plastic as she took in the brightly-lit scene.

Jean had her eyes closed, her head propped on a white pillow as she lay under sterile white sheets, an IV pole standing next to her with tubes connected to her veins. The harsh fluorescent lights accentuated the shocking mercurochrome color of her hair, which even though cropped short was sticking out in multiple directions looking like a medieval spiked weapon. Her face looked weathered and aged. Her once creamy porcelain skin was slightly yellowed. Jean looked shockingly different than any memory of her, which pushed Robin back a step while she gathered strength to move in closer.

The heavy door didn't make a sound when it closed so Nan leaned over the bed and whispered, "Are you awake, Jean? We're here."

In slow motion, Jean's eyelids fluttered open and adjusted to seeing Nan. Her eyes were bloodshot which made the dark brown irises look even more like the color of burnt toast. Nan moved closer to kiss her forehead gently.

"I brought someone with me." Robin moved tentatively into view. Jean stared blankly as if there was no recognition of her baby sister, the one her parents coddled and adored ad infinitum.

A million thoughts were pounding through Robin's brain. She hates me. How should I act around someone who tried to commit suicide? Who is this stranger? Woefully unstable, looking like death warmed over. Family.

"Hi Jean," was all Robin could manage to say in a small voice to which there was no reaction except for a continued glare. "How are you doing?," she added after a long silence.

"How does it look like I'm doing?" Jean sparred in a caustic tone.

"I've seen you looking better," Robin admitted with all the fortitude and honesty she could muster.

Nan interrupted the daggered look in Jean's dark chocolate eyes. "Robin came to help you."

"Too late," Jean snapped.

"Actually, it's just the beginning," Nan countered.

"I-I brought you something." Robin hesitatingly re-entered the verbal battle. She paused, rustled through her purse wishing she'd made Judy's creation more accessible instead of buried somewhere at the bottom. Her shoulders were so tense, her neck throbbed.

"Here!" Robin stepped closer, finally unearthing the bottle, and handing it out to Jean.

"What's that?" Jean eyeballed the offering suspiciously, leaving Robin with her arm awkwardly extended.

"My friend is an expert in aromatherapy, and she created this just for you. Try it. Roll it on your wrist and smell it."

Nan encouraged her. "It can't hurt, dear."

Both women watched as Jean gingerly accepted the gift, carefully removing the top. But with her arm restrained by the IV, she struggled until Nan moved in to help spread the concoction of rosemary, pine and cinnamon on her arm and her fingers. She raised her hand to her nose. Judy's combination was intended to reduce anger, discontentment, shame, and sadness.

"Smells like goddamn Christmas." Jean sniffed at the scents as if she were snorting cocaine.

Was that a good smell? Robin wondered.

"Makes me hungry." Jean looked directly into Robin's eyes which made Robin tense with concern. Suddenly her sister's gaze softened slightly. "Thank you, Robin. It's nice."

Relief poured through Robin's body in the form of warm pulsations which she could feel all the way to her feet. With lips pressed together, the sides of her mouth turned up slightly as she gave Jean a satisfied grin.

"You're welcome."

Robin and Nan stood uncomfortably by the side of the bed.

Nan finally asked, "May we sit?" Two durable, steel and vinyl beige-colored visitor chairs were waiting by the window on the far side of the bed.

"Yeah. Sure."

Robin scanned the room's monochromatic tones except for the pale blue blanket rolled neatly at the bottom of the bed. A television was suspended on one wall; on the other were beeping and flickering monitors and a chalkboard scrawled with time-checks of various nurses. A bedside table was wired with a call button and held a plastic water pitcher, a half-filled glass and the TV remote. A door on another wall led to a private bathroom. Everything was colored in soft, relaxing hues made less calming by the severe overhead fluorescents. A large window overlooked a parking lot surrounded by trees. The dark silvery sky was beginning to release raindrops which lightly pelted the pane.

As Robin bent her knees to sit, leaning forward slightly, her necklace fell forward. She grabbed at the silver locket and pushed it back against her chest. Jean watched and her expression changed.

"Wh-what are you doing with that?" Jean's voice was suddenly shrill and accusatory.

"What?," Robin asked innocently, feeling mild alarm.

"Th-the locket?"

Since Arles, Robin always wore the locket and she never thought about how her sister might react to seeing it, how it might trigger her. Jean was clearly agitated and for a reason which Robin was about to find out.

Trying to remain calm and collected Robin said, "It was mom's."

"I know it was mom's. I gave it to her."

Now it was Robin's turn to be gobsmacked as she felt a shockwave ripple through to the marrow of her bones. Like a house of cards, she feared she might collapse onto the hard floor.

"You gave it to mom," she repeated numbly in disbelief. "How…?"

Nan cut through the thick tensions, intervening in a steady voice. "Tell us about it, Jean. Your mom always wore that locket."

"Yeah. She did. Long story short. When Nathan and I got married…" Her voice cracked. "Mom was so happy for me and supportive. She did all the wedding planning…"

"It was beautiful," Robin said, remembering the lovely occasion that took place in a brownstone right off Gramercy Park, an elegant, intimate affair. Jean had looked like a fairytale bride in her long gown setting off her thick curls of red hair and peachy skin. Robin had just turned 19. Jean was 22.

"I never expected some of the things mom did. You know…we'd had our problems."

Robin squirmed.

"I wanted to show my appreciation. I found that antique locket…" Jean became emotional and paused so she could deliver the rest of the story. Robin and Nan waited in pregnant silence.

She talked directly to Robin. "It caught my eye in the window of a store in the village. After I bought it, I-I put a tiny photo of us as kids on one side and left the other side open for whatever she wanted to hold close to her." A tear escaped and rolled down Jean's cheek. She swiped at it with the back of her hand, brushing it away.

"I looked for it…after she…you know…went missing. I searched and searched…"

Robin was suddenly struck by guilt that she had her mother's locket and Jean didn't, the locket that had traveled to the South of France and landed in the protective hands of Marcel which Robin had been given and now wore always.

Nan relayed an abbreviated version how the necklace had turned up in a shop in France where Ruth had left it all those years ago. She omitted the part about Ruth intentionally leaving it there on the very day she vanished.

Robin's hands reached behind her neck for the clasp and undid the necklace. Her movements felt robotic as if she were being powered by an outside force and had little control over what she was doing. Holding each end in her fingers to create a V suspending the locket in the air, she got up and walked over to Jean. "It should be yours," she offered.

"No. No. That's okay. You went and found it. It looks good on you." Jean remembered the silly taunt when they were youngsters, finders keepers, losers weepers when one of them would claim the other's abandoned toy or crayon or candy.

"Are you sure?" Robin hesitated, but after Jean's firm nod of rejection, she returned it to her neck and sat. She wanted to ask Jean about the quote added to the locket. Does she know their mother's connection to Uriel Emanuel?

"What a lovely gesture," said Nan, looking into Jean's sad eyes. "Have you heard from Nathan?"

"Uh huh," she said softly.

"And…? Nan probed.

"I knew he'd gone to his sister's in Philly."

"You did? I thought you had no idea…" Nan stopped short seeing Jean bristle. "Go on," she urged.

"I called him. This morning." Her gaze turned to her IV tubes as the clear liquid was being pumped into her body. Then she raised her palms to her nose and took a long inhalation of the lingering scents.

"He's coming back."

"That's good news, isn't it?" Nan's voice encouraged Jean to continue talking.

"It is, but…" Her eyes filled with melancholy. She grappled with choosing to be honest or blaming him—and the world—for her unhappiness. She needed to own up to the pain that festered inside for years like a slow growing, undiagnosed cancer. The battle to face her fears showed in the deepening brow lines and slight tremulousness of her lower lip as she struggled. She stared out the window over the heads of Nan and Robin as if they weren't there. The pervasive silence was unnerving, made even more jarring by the beeping of electronics monitoring her vital signs.

Jean turned her head to look directly at her sister, which caused Robin's spine to stiffen like a steel rod. The storm outside seemed to have worsened at the same moment Robin's own turmoil was stirred up. The negative vibes between the sisters had dominated their relationship for so many years. Was it even possible to let them go? Could they eventually pass over like the dark clouds outside that would simply go away?

She sat tall, wishing there was something she could do to soften the moment, when Jean whispered, "I'm sorry," and without waiting for Robin's reaction, turned to Nan.

"The truth is, he left because I'm a mess. I was drinking. He wanted me to get help."

She closed her eyes and took another deep breath, exhaling with a loud sigh. She'd taken a first step of admission and nothing bad had happened. The hospital bed hadn't exploded. She was safe for the moment. She strained to raise her eyelids as if they weighed a ton. She turned to Nan.

"And now I am getting help," she said at last. "I'm ready. He's a good man. I need to become a better wife." More tears began to stream uncontrollably. "Sorry."

"No need to apologize. We're here to help. We love you." Nan got up, grabbed a tissue for Jean and lightly rubbed her arm.

Robin was overcome by emotions at seeing her sister's vulnerability, her grief. The sensations flooded down to her very core, mingling with a sense of possibility, a niggling hope for new beginnings for her sister and for herself. Maybe a relationship. Maybe she'd get her real sister back in her life?!

"When do you expect Nathan?," Nan asked gently.

"Tomorrow. I may even get released tomorrow."

"Good. We'll check with you tomorrow then. If you go home, may we visit there?"

"Yeah. Sure."

"We're going to visit the historic grist mill in the morning. It's on the National Register." She paused. "Unless you'll be home. We'll call you."

"Ok." Jean was visibly worn out from the visit.

"We should let you get some rest," suggested Nan.

Robin had been lost in thought. Nan's suggestion catapulted her back to the present. Nan was leaning over Jean giving her a peck on the cheek. Robin walked over, her legs wavering beneath her.

"May I give you a hug?," she asked in a puny voice. Jean responded by extending both arms, ready to receive Robin's affections, albeit stilted. Jean's bony body accepted the warmth. For Robin, the moment was both awkward and delicious. She could smell the scents of Judy's aromatherapy concoction and experienced an unusual blend of emotions explode inside her chest.

CHAPTER THIRTEEN

*J*ean was back home, relaxing on the living room couch, rapid firing the giant TV through channels as she sipped a cup of coffee. Nathan was in the kitchen humming to himself as he whipped up breakfast. He was cheerful when creating meals, even the simplicity of the day's first bite.

Nathan had done well as a successful accountant which afforded a beautiful waterfront, split level three-bedroom home in a great neighborhood in Long Island's Amityville. Jean appreciated their home, its sprawling open plan, solid hardwood floors, stone fireplace, and the spectacular views of the deep-water canal.

She could hear cooking noises—staccato chopping, pots clanging, water running—all emanating from the modern, well-equipped kitchen that had vaulted ceilings and a skylight. Her stomach rumbled from wafting smells of bacon and onions. She breathed in the sweet calmness in the moment. Jean never knew what the next minute would bring. She endured uninvited mood swings that took her on a roller coaster of emotions. She had expressed that she desperately wanted to get off the ride and to feel normal, whatever that was supposed to be.

Sunlight radiated into every room which should have given an uplifting outlook to the day. Instead, Jean struggled with frightening shadows from the depths of her being that threatened to engulf her in permanent blackness. The streaming sunshine covered up the darkness and made living a tiny bit more tolerable.

Before Nathan came into her life, long before they bought the luxurious house, she fought recurring internal demons. Unexpected bursts of emotions would erupt when she least expected them, like sudden spewing of molten lava. The mood swings started in college after the sexual entanglement with that boy Donald. The consequences changed her forever. Repressed feelings lodged in the cells of her violated body from the damaging illegal abortion. The inner wolves of shame and pain devoured her and sent her into withdrawal from life and from everyone she'd cared about, including her parents and her sister. Embarrassed to face her family, she ran away to deal with the "situation," as everyone euphemistically referred to it.

It took a few years, but she was able to climb out of the pits of despair and found Nathan, her savior and hero. When they got engaged, her mother came back into her life and actively planned and orchestrated the wedding. Ruth immediately accepted Nathan and loved his sweet attentiveness. Such a special time. A special mom-daughter relationship developed. Her mother became her understanding shoulder, a cautious confidante. Then abruptly and shockingly, it all changed again the very next year. Their relationship was tragically cut short when her mother vanished during the annual Triple Ts' trip.

Nathan never knew about the college incident as Jean was determined to bury that disgrace and forget. He steadfastly held her up and was consoling when her mother disappeared. He gave her hope that maybe her mother would be found. But, of course, she never was, and no one knew what happened, another blow to Jean's heart.

Over the years, the psychological pain from traumatic memories compounded by a childless marriage propelled her to self-medicate. Alcohol distorted her perceptions of reality. At first her drinking was socially acceptable at the club with the other ladies and she was outwardly functional. Afraid to admit to Nathan or herself that she had a problem, she began drinking alone, hiding in the bedroom when Nathan was at the office. It became out of control. Seeking professional help took a leap of faith, heightened by threats from Nathan to deal with her issues so they could enjoy their dreamlike existence. For Jean, it was never dreamlike. It was merely getting through and somehow being lucky enough to be tolerated by her husband with all her warts and insecurities.

She went through a revolving door of psychiatrists and medications, but nothing brought her stability or peace. The final trigger of collapse came when Nan called to invite her on the trip to revisit her mother's journey, a terrifying jump into the past. Robin would be going, too. Jean declined, upset and angry, retreating into a cocoon of sadness and depression, feeling empty, worthless and abandoned. Her drinking accelerated and Nathan complained that he wasn't going to stand around and watch her destroy herself. He packed his bags and left, seeking refuge with his sister in Philadelphia. His underlying wish was that his departure would knock sense into Jean, and she'd come around. Instead it sent her off the edge. She added old prescriptions to her alcohol, landing her on death's door in the psych ward at the local hospital.

Nathan was grateful to have her home now and prayed that this was the catalyst to propel her into recovery and healing. He had been so close to losing her forever and that would have been his unraveling. He kept himself together. He was a giver, generous to a fault. He reveled in doting on her, but she needed to do the heavy lifting. The truth was she wanted to be better as much as he wanted her to.

"What time did you say they were coming?," Nathan shouted as he puttered in front of the stove. He wore gray sweatpants and a green tee shirt. He had thinning light brown hair and a rounded face that gave him an amicable aura. He had a slight paunch on his 5'11" frame but otherwise appeared in shape.

"They said about noon," Jean answered in a loud voice.

"Good. Plenty of time to get in a bike ride." He emerged from the kitchen with two trays of plates artistically arranged with scrambled eggs, bacon, fruit slices, and sourdough toast. A lovely pink rose lay at the side of Jean's dish. Her face lit up.

"You're hired!" She looked up at him with admiration. She was wrapped in a comfortable white terrycloth robe with her flaming red hair slicked down. Her face was sagging with weariness from all the detoxing, but her eyes held a glimmer of light.

"I wasn't looking for a job," he quipped. "I'm looking for my wife to be healthy and happy."

His words were sincere and delivered with a warm smile, but they stung Jean. He noticed and wished he could retrieve the comment, but it was too late. Her body dejectedly hunched over the plate. She wasn't ready for the conversation she knew they needed to have. Now was not the time. Nan and Robin were due in a few hours and she wanted to present herself better than she was feeling. She picked at her eggs lethargically. Nathan sat beside her on the cream-colored leather couch.

"Are you up for taking a ride with me? We can make it a short one. Just to the beach and back." Nathan was trying so hard. She needed to attempt to reconnect with him.

"Sure. I'll need to get some clothes on."

"Really? You don't think the neighbors would want to see a white-robed damsel biking down the street?"

She chuckled at the comical image. Nathan possessed a quick-witted comedic humor that always made her laugh. She was glad he came back. She was ready to be home and would follow doctor's orders. She wanted to feel okay.

After the brief invigorating bike ride with Nathan, Jean was still upstairs getting dressed when Nan and Robin arrived. Nathan greeted the two women warmly at the door, now attired in casual khaki slacks and a blue polo. He directed them through the house to the outdoor deck. As they strolled through the luminous indoor spaces, both women craned their necks to absorb the well-decorated interiors, remarking how beautiful the home was. Nathan promised that Jean would give them a full tour but for now he showed them out to the wood-planked deck overlooking the dock and stunning water views.

"Oh wow," Robin gushed at the scene, not just eyeing the sparkling canal but also the generous assortment of drinks and snacks on the sleek round bistro table shaded by a dark red cantilevered umbrella. Nathan motioned for them to get comfortable on the red cushioned metal chairs.

"This is too much," Nan burbled.

The black and glass round tabletop was lavished with several glass pitchers of iced tea, orange juice and club soda. Colorful fruit cubes were adorned with decorative toothpicks. There was sesame hummus, a tray of raw vegetables, artisan crackers, a cheese plate, mini sandwiches of French bread with egg and chicken salads, and chocolate chip cookies. Little white dishes with black rims were stacked with spreading knives. Beside them were tall drink glasses and black cloth napkins.

"Quite an array," Robin remarked. "And the views…fabulous!"

"Do you have a boat?" Nan asked looking at the empty dock.

"No, but we have neighbors who do." Nathan grinned and quickly reacted to his wife appearing in the doorway. "There she is." He planted a kiss on her lips and pulled out a chair.

"Welcome to our humble abode. Has my husband been boring you with his stories?" Jean was a bit subdued but looked much better than she had in the hospital. Her flowing white blouse made a sharp contrast to her scarlet hair which was blown dry with short puffy curls. Her face was still tired and drawn but she managed a smile in the direction of Nan and Robin. The expression deepened the lines in her face and yet the corners of her eyes had an upward swoosh that gave her an odd air of contentment.

"Cute capris," Nan flattered, noticing Jean's rainbow-dotted white pants. "You look really good today."

She responded with a curt "thanks" and glanced into the still channel of blue-green waters extending beyond sight. She seemed to sink into moodiness and yet there was a subtle ease as she enjoyed the company and being outdoors.

"So, what may I serve you?" Nathan filled the sharp silence, waving at the drinks asking no one in particular.

Robin spoke first. "Iced tea for me, please. Is it sweetened or unsweetened?"

"Unsweetened," replied Nathan as he shoveled ice into a glass and poured the dark tea.

"Perfect. I like my tea neat," she said and then wished she hadn't used any reference to alcohol. She steered away from looking at her sister who was not acknowledging the comment as she continued staring off into the canal.

"I'll have the same," said Nan.

Jean sighed loudly and then casually requested, "My usual. Half orange juice, half seltzer."

"Oh wait," Nan reconsidered. "That sounds more refreshing. I'll have one of those too. What a great combination!"

"My honey's favorite!" While Nathan poured the drinks, he encouraged everyone to help themselves to food.

Jean sipped her drink silently as she watched everyone plating up their snack choices.

"Jean tells me you went to visit the mill this morning. Was it worth the tour?," Nathan asked. "I've never been."

Nan and Robin stumbled over each other as they described the fascinating visit to the authentic early American grist mill built in 1751 which surprisingly still functioned. They were amazed to be able to watch a miller grind and make flour and were fortunate to meet the man who runs the place.

"He's a retired aerospace engineer with expansive knowledge about the history out here. I'm wondering if I can get assigned to write about it," said Robin.

Jean looked squarely at her sister. "You're still writing?" Her voice was oddly edgy.

"I've never stopped." Robin couldn't read Jean. Was she admiring my profession or judging me in a bad way? Was she jealous? Or critical? Not wanting to trigger her sister in any way, she resisted pursuing the subject, but it seemed like an unwanted wedge between them.

Nathan was an excellent host, cordial and entertaining. He had a keen wit and kept the conversation fun and lively. They discussed the peaceful neighborhood and how they'd found this gem of a house, with the nearby ocean beaches and Gatsby-style mansions, the good local economy, and the weather. Jean was overtly quiet. It was a lovely sunny summer day with long streaks of white clouds strewn across the blue skies, and slight humidity offset by a gentle breeze.

"Sometimes July can be unbearable," noted Nathan.

From a birds-eye view, the four adults appeared almost like a normal family, gathering on a weekend in the seasonal outdoors to enjoy the day and catch up with one another. But it was far from typical. It was as if there were a giant gorilla standing beside the deck ready to pounce at the least provocation. No one had the courage to ask how Jean was feeling or what was next in her recovery. No one ventured into any discussion of the recent trip to the South of France. Everyone tiptoed around conversations that could potentially spark Jean into a meltdown, distancing themselves from any statement that might make her uncomfortable. They could sense how raw she was. But the reality was that not talking about the status of her mental state made the visit strained and difficult. Robin was beginning to sense that coming to New York had been a waste of time. She wasn't getting any closer to mending the rift that gaped between them and it seemed there was little she could do to help Jean.

Impatient with the chit-chat, Robin finally ventured forth with the question that burned inside her since the locket incident at the hospital. In a cautious voice, she asked Jean, "Have you ever heard of Uriel Emanuel?" She held her breath as the question hung in the air. Jean looked skyward searching her memory. Robin waited patiently.

"It sounds familiar, but I can't place it," Jean finally replied. Noticing Robin's obvious disappointment, she repeated the name a few times aloud. "Hmmmm. If I remember, I'll let you know."

"Mom might've known him." Robin saw a flicker in Jean's eyes and was hesitant to say more.

The afternoon dissolved into early evening. They had gotten the full tour of the house, consumed all the food, talked about everything acceptable under the sun, and realized it was time to go. Nathan invited them to stay for dinner, but they protested. They were stuffed and could see that Jean was fatigued to the point she needed to lie down. They agreed to return for a brief goodbye in the morning before Nan would drive Robin to catch an evening flight back to Florida. Jean said nothing as they left but gave both women a cursory hug.

On the car ride to the mill that morning, Robin had discussed with Nan whether staying any longer made any sense. She complained she wasn't sleeping well. The hotel bed was too soft, and she awoke several times with throbbing aches from the injuries from the motorcycle accident. She thought she had healed but now she was hurting. She'd popped a few ibuprofens to get back to sleep but the night had been full of disquieting dreams.

In one, she saw a younger version of herself at her childhood home, walking alone to the beach which was a few houses away. She could hear the crashing of ocean waves. As she got closer to the sand and gazed out at the agitated Atlantic, she caught a glimpse of shocking red hair bobbing on the surface. She couldn't see a body or a face. And then the carrot top slipped beneath a roaring wave and never reappeared. She awoke with a start and her body was in pain.

In another dream, she and her sister were kids, riding together on ancient cobblestoned roads, bumping along laughing. Robin couldn't recognize the location, but it seemed old and foreign. Suddenly, a car appeared out of nowhere and careened headlong into the bicycle her sister was riding. In horror, Robin screamed but the sounds wouldn't come out of her throat. She felt like she was suffocating and then woke up in a pool of perspiration. After the fitful night, Robin was bone weary.

Nan's opinion was that Robin had made the effort to travel all this way to see her sister and that was enough for now. She had given Jean a signal that she cared. Both sisters needed time to digest and assimilate what had transpired and what might unfold next. In the meantime, she wanted to get home to ready for the workshop in Miami. Nan smiled and patted Robin's thigh in a motherly way that communicated acceptance and love.

The new morning was more humid, and the skies were dreary. It was 10 when Robin and Nan were greeted by Nathan before they even rang the doorbell. He ushered them into the living room where Jean was stretched out on the couch, eyes closed.

"Sorry, she had a bad night," whispered Nathan. He leaned over Jean, giving her a peck on the forehead. "Honey, Nan and your sister are here to see you."

Eyes fluttered open and a smile spread slowly across her sad-looking face, lending a cheerier appearance.

"Good morning." Nan leaned in to give an awkward hug.

"Hi." Robin reached out to squeeze Jean's hand.

Nathan asked if they'd like coffee or tea. "I've got fresh scones direct from the bakery."

"Coffee for me, please," replied Robin. She was fond of Nathan and his generous nature. He had a warmth for people, atypical for an accountant who was usually more focused on numbers.

"Make yourselves comfortable." Nathan gestured to the loveseat and plush armchairs perpendicular to the couch.

"If it's no trouble, I'd prefer tea," said Nan, choosing a comfortable chair. "So how are you today?" She directed her question to Jean.

"Okay. Just didn't sleep too well."

"I can relate," chirped Robin who plopped down on the loveseat. She rambled on about her accident and how her body seemed to default into pain mode from time to time and the hotel bed didn't help matters.

"We didn't know about your accident. Lucky you're alive. You could've stayed with us," Nathan chimed in. "Jeanie honey, would you like tea or coffee?"

"We were absolutely fine staying at the hotel," offered Nan, giving Robin a distressed glance for her blathering.

"Tea, please," said Jean as Nathan headed for the kitchen. Wisps of Jean's red hair stuck out of a brightly colored decorative scarf she had wrapped tightly around her head like a turban. It gave her an exotic look. She wore classic denim shorts topped with a white tee shirt adorned with an abstract green and orange design emblazoned with the word RESOLVE.

"What's RESOLVE?," asked Robin pointing to Jean's shirt.

Jean looked down at her chest, forgetting what she'd put on that morning. "Oh, it's an organization to help abused women."

"Is it a shelter?," asked Nan.

"No. It's a non-profit that offers free counseling to women who are in bad home situations. They learn about options for themselves and their children. They can even apply for money to get out on their own, get job training. For my donation, I got this shirt."

"I like it," said Nan.

"Sounds worthwhile," said Robin as she gazed around, taking in the full interior of the living room: a floor-to-ceiling flagstone fireplace on one side, a beautiful bay window overlooking the canal on the other. A warm cocoa and beige oriental area rug pulled together the tasteful oversized furnishings. Sleek modern wooden end tables were dramatically contrasted by a vintage solid distressed-wood cocktail table with a rust-hued lock and handle that opened to an inside storage compartment, reminiscent of French country style. A few oversized elegant books graced the surface next to the small aromatherapy vial, which Robin was pleased to see had a place of prominence. Artistically placed knickknacks were carefully arranged on various surfaces. The free-form flow of the space was pleasing. Robin especially liked the hardwood floors.

"RESOLVE formed about three years ago, and they've already reached so many. I was glad to contribute." Jean worked her way into a seated position, looking the most animated since arriving home. "I have something for you," she changed the subject, speaking to Robin. "I found this." She stretched out her hand to pick up a hardbound book from an end table and haltingly extended it to her younger sister.

Robin accepted and stared at the aging rumpled dustcover, unable to believe her eyes. She blinked to clear her vision. Jean had just given her a book by Uriel Emanuel. Her heart started racing.

"I knew the name rang a bell. It was in mom's stuff. I hadn't looked in those piles in years, but I remembered this book." Jean fluffed a foam couch pillow behind her head. "It stood out because it's signed to her."

"What?!" Robin couldn't conceal her astonishment. "Autographed. How?" She opened the cover to read aloud a pen-written inscription: "To Ruth, Honored to have you as one of my first students. May this book remind you of new beginnings. Love and Light, Uriel."

"Synchronicity," Nan exclaimed, pulling modestly at her skort which had hiked up when she'd sat on the extra deep cushion. She was the matron of the group and carried herself with a distinct elegance, a warm, compassionate personality that aligned appropriately with her psychotherapy work.

"Holy moly," exclaimed Robin. "May I borrow it? I'll mail it back to you after I've read it." She read the title aloud: *How to Live Your Dream Life.*

"Yeah, sure. Take it. But I want it back." A slight tension made Jean's tone harsh.

"I'll send it back as soon as I finish reading it. Is that okay?"

"Okay."

Robin continued to explore the book. "I'm stunned…Wow…. It was published in the early nineties."

"I was pretty stunned when I found it," said Jean. "Never knew mom did stuff like that."

Nathan re-entered the room holding a tray of hot drinks and scones which he laid on the coffee table.

"Ladies, please help yourselves." He settled himself next to his wife and picked up a coffee. "What kind of stuff are you talking about?" Nathan wanted to know, entering mid-conversation.

"Self-development, self-empowerment," said Robin. "Learning from a spiritual influencer. He lives in New York and teaches workshops all over the world about connecting to your earthly mission… Sheesh, he must've been in his early twenties when mom went to him."

"Probably was just starting out," Nan suggested. "Ruth never mentioned him."

"So odd." Robin shook her head.

"That's why Robin is heading home tonight. She's registered for a workshop he's teaching in Miami in a few days." Nan sipped her tea nonchalantly.

"No kidding?!," exclaimed Nathan. "Well that's a bizarre coincidence."

Both Nan and Robin knew it wasn't quite a coincidence but neither wanted to elaborate. Robin was slightly annoyed at Nan for mentioning the workshop. It was a violation of her privacy. She hadn't wanted to share that information publicly, at least not yet and not with her sister. So, she quickly re-focused attention. "Looks like you're using the oils that my friend mixed for you," she said as she pointed to the blue-labeled vial on the table.

"Yeah. I like the smell." Jean reached for it and dabbed some on her wrist, then sucked in an exaggerated breath.

"Good. That's good," said Robin, carefully spreading butter and jam on a scone, balancing it on a napkin in her lap. She couldn't wait to tell Judy how well her potion had worked and what a great gift it had been.

Out of the blue, Nathan asked Nan, "How's your husband doing?"

"Actually, he's thinking of retiring. But I'm not sure he's the retiring type. His patients have been his life."

"I don't believe in retirement," Robin announced.

"Well you have a long way to go, my dear," chided Nan. "You don't have to think about it."

"I mean, when you love what you do why would you stop? I've seen older people go into decline when they give up their work. It's their purpose."

"She has a point," said Nathan.

"He is a surgeon, you know. At some point, the hands aren't as steady to hold that scalpel and with plastic surgery... well... it could be disastrous," said Nan.

"Yeah, you wouldn't want some woman ending up with a face like a monkey." Nathan laughed to himself. "Sorry, Nan. Just sayin."

Robin couldn't contain herself. "Don't some start out that way? And then he fixes them? Just sayin." She joked and then accidentally inhaled a crumb of her scone and started coughing. Through the mild choking, she managed, "Guess I deserve to gag on my words…"

"Okay, you two…" Nan smirked and raised her teacup as if she were toasting their comments.

Suddenly, completely out of the flow of conversation, Jean said, "I'd like to go…"

"Go where, dear? You don't need surgery."

"I'd like to go to a workshop. Not now, but maybe someday soon." She looked at Nathan expectantly, hoping he might pick up the thread. But Nathan was focused on buttering his scone. "Maybe you'd go with me?"

Nathan looked up in surprise. "Really? You mean this guru person? That interests you?"

"Well if this guy was good enough for my mother…" She looked away. "Maybe it can help."

Robin jumped in. "He may have programs in the city. I mean, he's based here. Why don't I let you know what it's like after I've gone? Then you can decide if it makes sense for you."

"That's a good suggestion," said Nathan.

Jean did not react.

The room was uncomfortably quiet until Nathan asked the time of Robin's flight.

"Not 'til 8:55."

Nan filled the gap, explaining that they'd just made plans to drive into the city to meet Stephanie for a late lunch, and then she'd drop Robin back at JFK.

CHAPTER FOURTEEN

*O*n the flight back to the Fort Myers airport, Robin nestled into a window seat and reflected on her strange visit, feeling a persistent sadness. Her sister's image came to mind, a tortured stranger. The peculiar red hair, her face lined with drug and alcohol abuse, her depression and manic moods. The distance between them was not just physical in where and how they lived. Sure, they were blood relatives—and the only ones left in their familial line—but that seemed to be the only commonality. The sister of childhood no longer existed; that connection was gone. But perhaps a different relationship was emerging. A definite highlight of the trip, besides spending time with Nan and seeing Stephanie, was borrowing the book that belonged to her mother, the book that gave additional insight into this powerful man who was so influential, who had made a serious impression on her mother and who she'd be meeting in a few days. Now she had two books; the one from Marcel was clearly a more recent publication.

More thoughts pummeled through her brain. The Amityville house was enviable, and she got to know Nathan a little better. A burst of jealousy rose like a small fire in her chest, a hot flame that burned at her emotions. How had her sister managed to attract such an adoring husband? Jean was broken. What could she offer him? A streak of guilt momentarily flashed through her system for the harsh judgment. She should be happy for her sister. Nathan was devoted to Jean. Even though he had temporarily left her, his desperate move was a calculation, hoping to shock her into going into rehab and recovery so they could have a life.

It was Nathan's unconditional love for Jean that made Robin wonder what that might feel like in her own life, to have someone so caring. She questioned why she didn't have such a relationship. Her thoughts twisted to Richard, followed by a surge of anger as she envisioned him living with another man in Paris. Then a stream of consciousness took her to an image of Adam. What about the musician? She'd had a pleasant lunch with him. He seemed smart and interesting. Maybe he's relationship material? She stopped her spinning mind and laughed at herself. Hold on, she told herself. One lunch. I had one damn lunch with him.

She told herself to stop feeling alone and desperate. So what if I'm 45. She knew girlfriends who'd met their soulmates much later in life. Perhaps there was still hope for her. She was too needy and empty. Maybe I need a dog? Nah, too much responsibility. Maybe goldfish? Nah, they die too quickly.

She searched her mind for an idea, a plan, something that would give her joy and allow her to feel whole and complete within herself. She was ghosting through life not truly living it. She could work on being alone without feeling lonely. What can I change? What can I do to feel better?

Just then, the plane touched ground with a bump, and it rocked her into the present. Time to re-enter what was suddenly feeling like a pitiful, lonely existence. No one was available to pick her up. She understood. She hit the phone app for Uber. I can handle life.

Before entering the house, she pulled her mail out of the box stationed at the curb. The condo was deadly quiet. She felt hollow. Maybe a warm bath would lift her spirits but first she'd check her email. On second thought, I should check the mail, probably some bills I've neglected.

On top of the pile of ad circulars and solicitations for power washing and pizza deliveries sat a pink envelope with colorful stamps from France, her address scrawled in ink. A chill ran down her spine as she pulled out a handwritten letter from Marcel's daughter, Michelle

Ruth. Four pages were filled with newsy perspectives of a teenager in Arles. She was happy to report that her cast came off and she was back in action. She complained about her father being too strict, especially since she'd be turning 16 in just a few weeks. But she knows he means well. She'd met a boy in one of her classes, who is conspiring with her on a project to create an interactive app for kids to air their parental concerns. A kind of "Dear Abby" for kids. Michelle was writing a lot for her school newspaper on local activities but yearned to write for public journals or online magazines. She asked Robin for recommendations on how someone her age could break into a professional writing career. "Maybe," she ventured, "I could write for a publication in the U.S. reporting from France?"

Robin was impressed with Michelle's ability to express herself in English and was touched that the youngster had followed up on the offer to become long-distance pen pals. A warm glow filled her momentarily until she came back to face her own reality of the evening's solitude. Leaving the letter strewn on her kitchen counter, she decided she'd write back in the morning. Now it was bath time.

~

The bright Florida sunshine poured through Robin's window, forcing her awake. She glanced wearily at the clock. Seeing it was almost eight, she sat bolt upright. She never slept past seven. Her mind scanned information. I'm home. What day is it? What do I need to do? Then like a bolt of lightning electrifying her consciousness and memory cells, she remembered the trip, her sister, the sadness, and it sent her back onto the pillow. Okay, I've got to get up and face the day.

Finally, with a cup of coffee in one hand and her phone in the other, wrapped in a silky peach bathrobe, she slid open the glass door to her lanai and stepped out into the warm tropical air. She took a deep inhalation of the sweet, humid air and tucked herself into a chair at the outdoor table in the cool shade of a palm tree. She sipped the strong black liquid, feeling it slink down her throat, its caffeine beginning to liven her senses. Her phone displayed a text from Judy marked urgent. She hurriedly hit the call button.

Judy sounded frantic, unlike her usual easygoing self. She wanted to hear about Robin's sister but first she was dealing with an emergency and it affected Robin. Her right-hand assistant at Golden Moon had been rushed to the hospital with appendicitis and would be out for at least a week. There was no way Judy could get away for the Miami workshop. She was exceedingly apologetic. After all, she'd talked Robin into going and she regretted having to bail at the last minute. But this could not be resolved in time. Was there someone else Robin wanted to ask?

Robin thought for a beat. Her sister? Jean had said she wanted to go to a workshop but on second thought, Robin couldn't bear the idea, the intrusion, the moodiness. Guilt stuck in her throat as she pictured her sister's presence as an unwanted burden. She quickly rationalized that Jean was probably not recovered enough to travel.

"No." Robin's voice was shallow and full of defeat. "There's no one. I'll just go by myself."

"Are you okay?"

"I will be. I'm sorry about your assistant."

"Anything I can do?"

"No. I'll probably go a day earlier since I have to do research for that story on the art district."

"I'm really sorry, Robin. You know I'd do whatever I could if I could go."

"I know."

"Let's have dinner before you go. We need to catch up. A lot seems to be happening."

"You can say that again. Sure, let's meet tomorrow. Aurelio's?"

"Sounds perfect. 6:30?"

"It's a date."

"Love you."

Robin ended the call and felt a giant tidal wave of aloneness wash over her body. Then she remembered the letter from Michelle Ruth and decided to distract herself by writing a response.

~

Two days later, Robin was speeding across Alligator Alley toward Miami, bouncing to the streaming music of Lady Gaga. She would arrive too early to check into her hotel, so she decided to go directly to the art district and poke around galleries. Her dinner with Judy had been an excellent release for both. They had talked for hours but they also had way too much wine and she was now a little rough around the edges. The thumping music was keeping her energies flowing, helping her stay focused on the highway.

Robin arrived before noon at Reflections Art Gallery, a sleek, modern two-story showcase for emerging and established contemporary artists located in the heart of the art district. She ventured inside the attractive, high-ceilinged building, deciding to begin touring on the second floor. Ascending the broad stairs, she inconspicuously pulled at the hem of her short denim skirt so as not to be too revealing. She wore a light pink blouse and her favorite dangling silver earrings. Halfway up the stairs, she paused to adjust the slipped heel strap on her wedged sandals, requiring that she lay her multi-colored, open-top tote on the step. As she did, she realized she'd probably chosen quite an impractical artist-made purse for city travels. Too late! After the shoe adjustment, she bent down to retrieve her bag. The forward bend mildly activated a hangover headache she'd been fighting.

A young couple stood by a sculpture in a corner, so Robin headed toward the exhibit of vibrant paintings by Mexican artists. Abstract splashes of oil graced the canvas next to oblongs of solid colors with a single centered circle in a contrasting color. A few watercolor scenes of farmlands and mountains were presented by a South American painter. Continuing along the wall, she came upon black-and-white landscape photographs in large formats that were breathtaking. She reached in her bag for her phone and made a note of the artist's name. The upstairs level featured mostly emerging artists. She tapped in a few other artists' names, then turned to descend the stairs to the exhibition titled "Synchronicity," representing more established artists.

About halfway down her shoe strap slipped again causing her to stumble. While catching her balance, she lost hold of her purse and watched in utter helplessness as it went careening down the steps in painful slow motion, emptying all its contents in a heap at the landing. As happenstance would have it, a heart-stopping, good-looking man had been watching her descend and was now kneeled beside her belongings, gathering and shoving them back into her tote. How absolutely embarrassing.

She felt as if her insides were exposed all over the gallery floor. She swooped in, thanking the gentleman with tousled dark hair for his kindness. He looked into her eyes and smiled, sending a ripple of excitement down her spine. He was a slightly older version of Bradley Cooper, scruffy face, a touch of silver at his temples and soft blue eyes. He had a rugged, street-smart way of dressing in a kind of urban jungle explorer outfit, a hemp long-sleeved khaki shirt casually rolled up, lightweight trousers and tan lace-up urban suede oxfords. She guessed he was about 50.

He gently took her elbow and guided her to a standing position.

"Well, that was quite the entrance!" she said, meekly straightening her skirt and tossing her tote over her shoulder.

He laughed softly.

"Thank you." She found herself dissolving into his handsome face.

"My pleasure." He turned toward the exhibition. "Have you viewed the works yet?"

"No, I was just about to when I unexpectedly decided to have my own exhibition…of all the innards of my purse." She grinned and allowed his hand to remain supportively on her elbow.

"May I?" He directed her to the first wall of stunning abstract square oil paintings in complementary vibrant colors arranged three deep in rows of six. Each segment was a mirror of the next which gave the display an overall visual rhythm.

"Very striking." Robin looked up at him, figuring he was almost six feet tall. "Do you know the artist?"

"Funny you should ask. He's my neighbor in New York. So, yes, I know him. Jonathan Gee. Incredibly talented."

"Where do you live in New York?" She felt the heat of his hand penetrating her arm, burning through her skin.

When he told her near Washington Square Park, an eruption of conversation ensued about the city. Robin shared her former village lifestyle and how much she missed the culture of New York. She became animated and bubbly. When he asked where she lives now, she replied, "The other coast."

He pushed further. "Where in California?"

Robin giggled, realizing she should be more explicit. "Not that other coast, although I did once live in Westwood. But I live in Naples, on the west coast of Florida, just across the state."

"Ah yes, I've been to Naples. Beautiful!"

"So, do you know any of the other artists here?"

"No. But I'm enjoying the work." He continued to guide her, noticing that she was occasionally making notes on her phone. "Are you an art buyer?"

"Not really. More a connoisseur. Actually, I'm a journalist. I'm doing a story on the art district."

"Great! You should interview the owner. An interesting story in his own right and an excellent artist. He's out of town for a few days but he'd be worth talking to."

"Thanks for the tip. I'll be sure to follow up. By the way, I'm Robin."

"Nice to meet you Robin. My friends call me Yuri."

As they finished exploring the gallery, Yuri invited her to join him for lunch. "There's a nice bistro around the corner, The Good & Plenty Café. It's a farm-to-fork menu that's really good and good for you." The headache that had plagued Robin earlier had miraculously vanished under the attention of this charming man.

The casual low-key restaurant had a friendly atmosphere as they settled into a booth with a window view, but all Robin could concentrate on was Yuri. He had a self-assured intelligence that was almost professorial. He oozed a sexiness that was disarming. He seemed to have it all, smarts, good looks. Yet instead of being egocentric, he continually asked Robin questions about herself with sincere interest. He seemed to enjoy hearing about her motorcycling adventures and showed authentic compassion when she mentioned the accident.

Finally, her attention turned to the menu with its vast range of healthy choices.

"Food is medicine," said Yuri. "You are what you eat."

"What do you mean?"

"Food is information, messages to the body. I've prevented and reversed diseases through nutrition."

"Sounds like you speak from experience."

"It happened when I was incredibly young. I got sick, had a low-grade fever and doctors couldn't figure out the source. They called it a fever of unidentified origin. I was ill, isolated in bed for months. Then my mother got this bright idea to change the foods I was eating. That was the beginning of my healing."

"Wow."

"It was a low point for me. But I believe we learn and grow from adversity. It forces us in certain directions." He glanced at the menu.

"So, what do you recommend?," Robin asked, overwhelmed by all the options.

"Depends. What do you like?" The handsome stranger's eyes scanned her face. She felt pulled to him. She liked him. But food-wise, she didn't really care.

"I'm open. I'm thinking lentil soup, hummus and a side salad."

"You must try the sweet potato cake. I'll order one to share."

She was reminded once again of her mother's advice that a boy who shares his lunch is preferable to one who steals your lunch. They ordered.

Without warning, a question blurted out of Robin's mouth, "How long are you here?"

Yuri laughed, a deep-throated unrestrained reaction that was contagious. Robin convulsed into laughter, tears staged in the corners of her eyes, but she was unsure why she was laughing, except the moment seemed funny. She dabbed at the water droplets with her napkin, trying to catch her breath.

"Sounds like an existential question," Yuri stated after the guffaws subsided. "You mean in Miami?"

"Yes. Sorry. For a communicator, I'm not being clear, am I?"

"I'll be staying a couple of days, possibly longer. It depends."

Yuri did not elaborate any further.

Now it was Robin's turn to be taken by surprise when Yuri asked if she was free for dinner tomorrow. He was tied up today and would be busy until about 5:30 tomorrow but perhaps they could dine together around 6:30.

Robin quickly calculated that the workshop ended at five tomorrow evening, so she could conceivably accept the invitation. She nodded affirmatively. In her gut she felt ping-pong-like balls of joy bouncing in all directions. "I'd like that."

"Where are you staying? I'll pick you up," he offered.

"In the Art Deco area. The Clevelander on South Beach."

Yuri looked mildly surprised. "Synchronicity…" he said.

"Like the exhibit?"

"Yes, definite synchronicity. I'm at the same hotel, so that'll make it easier."

"What are the chances!" Robin exclaimed.

"Carl Jung called it meaningful coincidences. I call it divine mindfulness. So, let your intuitive awareness open," he advised. She shuddered, flashing on the words that Hannah the psychic had spoken not too long ago.

In what seemed like an amazingly fast turnaround, the waiter delivered their meals. As they ate, they chatted about the lifestyle in Miami and the influences of the Cuban and South American cultures.

"Are you someone who likes surprises?," Yuri asked and seemed to be analyzing her reactions.

"I do. The unexpected can be fun. Why do you ask?" She could not hide her puzzled expression which caused Yuri to chuckle, but he gave no answer. Instead, he planted his large protective fingers to cover her smooth, petite hand that was casually perched on the table. "You're such a delightful, delicate flower," he remarked, and without waiting for Robin to respond he announced, "I have a meeting I need to get to. May I escort you back to the gallery?" He settled the bill discreetly, waving away Robin's gesture towards her purse.

Robin didn't need escorting. Her car was parked closer to the restaurant than the gallery. If ending their lunch abruptly was Yuri's idea of a surprise, then she didn't like surprises very much. Fatigue was beginning to descend over her mind and body so she decided the other galleries could wait until later. She'd drive over and check into the hotel, take a swim or a warm bath and maybe even a nap. She thanked Yuri profusely for rescuing her scattered possessions at the gallery, for a lovely and healthy lunch, and told him how much she was looking forward to seeing him tomorrow evening.

Before they parted, he pulled her to him and hugged her, embracing with such intensity that it startled her. Unprepared, she stiffened slightly.

"I'm a hugger," he confessed. "Hugs are good for the spirit. See you tomorrow evening." With that, he spun on his heels and walked away, leaving Robin stupefied. Am I dreaming? What a crazy encounter.

The rest of the day, all she could think about was Yuri, the hug, his touch, his suave good looks, his generosity, and wisdom. Get a grip, she told herself. I have an article to research and a workshop to attend.

CHAPTER FIFTEEN

*T*he next morning, she got up early to practice yoga in her room. After showering, feeling cleansed by the thumping of the delightful, high-pressure showerhead, Robin put on black leather-looking yoga pants, a short-sleeved white tee shirt, and a light black-and-white jacket to protect against the air-conditioned ballroom where the workshop was taking place. She wore black ballet flats with attention towards comfort. After all, it was expected to be a long day. She grabbed her arty purse and threw in her phone along with the borrowed book from her sister, the one autographed by the well-known presenter with whom she was hoping to connect at some point over the weekend. Unfortunately, she'd not had any time to read any of it nor the other book from Marcel. But perhaps she'd get a chance to ask the author about this book, and if perhaps he remembered her mother.

She treated herself to a sumptuous breakfast in the sophisticated trendy lounge with tabletops in varying vibrant colors, walls decorated with contemporary artwork. She chose a neon green high-top isolated in a far corner where she could observe the comings and goings while feeling protected against a wall.

As she and Yuri had discussed, Miami reminded her of an urban melting pot of influences from all over the world, stimulating and engaging, fun and exciting. It didn't have the edginess of New York City, but it had its own dynamics of culture, tropical colors, loud salsa music, texture, and a light fiesta mindset. It wouldn't be her choice as a place to live but the area was certainly entertaining. The Art Deco

Historic District, which surrounded the hotel, captivated her. It was full of impressive architectural sites.

The last time she visited Miami's Art Deco area was with Richard. It was their first trip together and they had stayed with Richard's friends in a fabulous home on Key Biscayne overlooking the brilliant sandy beach. One of the days, they drove over on their motorcycles to explore all along Ocean Drive and Collins Avenue. She remembered gawking at the whimsical ornamentations, exotic fountains, geometric statues, and facades of pastels from blues to pinks to bright oranges and yellows. The structural gems dated back to the 1920s and 30s and she enjoyed all the glamorous embellishments, the shiny curves, glass blocks, chrome accents, and terrazzo floors. For Richard, it was a far cry from the Art Deco places he was familiar with in Paris, where the style had originated, but he was amused by the tropical interpretations. She missed Richard's European sensibilities. She fought against her darkening mood, feeling abandoned and rejected by his recent homosexual choice. Move on, she counseled herself. Tomorrow, instead of yoga stretching, she'd start with a brisk early morning walk for a visual Art Deco extravaganza. It would be far more exhilarating, and she could bury old memories of Miami and create new ones.

~

The program was starting at nine with registration opening at eight. At about 8:30 a.m., Robin sauntered to the reception area filled with clusters of people who, like her, were checking in and collecting a badge and materials. Her workbook was entitled, *Recharge. Rewire. Reconnect. Learn to activate your authentic power. Create the life you deserve now.*

She was ready. She strolled to a seat towards the front of the hall. Closing her eyes, she slowed her breath and asked for guidance in getting the most out of this experience. Using Yuri's eloquent words from the day before, she requested divine mindfulness.

At exactly nine, a tall blonde woman looking to be in her twenties took to the microphone to greet the packed ballroom of about

500 attendees. She asked everyone to release all expectations and surrender to the experience. "The more you let go, the more you will be open to receive," she said and gathered her hands at her heart. In the next breath it was her great honor and privilege to introduce Uriel Emanuel. She gave a brief biographical profile and then asked the audience to give a heartfelt welcome to this humble and amazing spiritual leader. A handsome dark-haired man appeared, his image projected on a giant screen covering the entire back wall of the stage. The camera followed him.

Robin watched with rapt attention as *her Yuri* strutted out onto the stage. "Oh my God," she gasped audibly, causing her seatmates to shoot her an annoyed glance. She almost fell out of her chair into a bundle of nerves on the floor as her jaw dropped in astonishment. He never mentioned why he was in Miami and she never thought to ask. Some journalist I am! I should've known Yuri is short for Uriel.

She was off balance or maybe it was the hangover headache. But there he was, larger than life, occupying the grand platform with masterful authority. He scanned the audience to make contact with the many faces, and then he lit on hers, pausing abruptly. He beamed a surprised yet energetic smile at her, lingering for what seemed like a century. She felt the corners of her mouth turn up. Noticing his gaze, hundreds of attendees craned their necks to see who he was acknowledging so intently.

Robin felt every hair on her body stand at attention. Realizing she'd stopped breathing, she sucked in a gulp of air to steady herself.

Uriel addressed the audience, his blue eyes communicating compassion and intelligence on the enormous screen. He encouraged the attendees to sit back and relax, and open to the light and information he would be sharing over the next 48 hours. He re-emphasized the blonde's recommendations. "The more you surrender to the experiences of today and tomorrow, the more you will benefit." He spoke in a calm, melodic voice that bordered on hypnotic.

Yuri wore the same tan slacks and oxfords that she remembered from yesterday. He looked striking in a blue button-down oxford shirt that made his eyes appear even bluer, but maybe it was the pixel effect of the enlarged screen image. Or maybe it was her distorted perceptions. It was hard not to be distracted by his inescapable attractiveness, his smooth-shaven chiseled cheeks and chin, lean and fit body, and the animated gestures. Character lines on his face etched a story of contentment; his crow's feet conveyed smiles of joy. Robin wrestled with her mind to stay focused on the brilliance of his messages. She kept drifting off into swirling thoughts when she suddenly became aware that everyone was standing and the person on her left was introducing herself.

Caught off-guard, Robin mumbled an apology to this noticeably big woman. She had completely tuned out and didn't catch the instructions that had obviously been imparted to the crowd. The robust, cherubic-faced dark-skinned participant dressed in a frilly purple blouse towered over Robin, and explained that everyone was given a minute to tell the person next to them who they were and what they want for the future. "He said we're all in this together and to meet and accept one another in this moment."

"So…" She paused to extend her arm for a business-like handshake. "I'm Teresa Sanchez. I'm a single mom of two fabulous little girls. I live here in Miami. I work in banking. I'm a bank teller. But I'm hoping to change careers. I'm studying to be a physician's assistant and I'll graduate next year. I want to make a difference for my kids, and I want to be able to buy a house. I want to help people. A better life." She ended her shotgun delivery, breathing heavily. "Admirable goals," Robin nodded robotically without emotion. She felt like she'd had an out-of-body experience and was trying to get back to her physical center.

"Oh, my turn, I guess… I'm Robin Stevens. I'm divorced. I live in Naples. I'm a journalist." She thought about what she hoped for and was stymied. What do I want? A loud voice, *his voice*, directed everyone to wrap it up. Thirty seconds remained. Robin blurted, "I don't know what I want. Maybe to find my purpose and be happy with who I am." As the words flowed out, there was a pang of awkwardness after accidentally admitting insecurities. She'd aired her secret of paralyzing emotional blockages. She wanted to let go but an inner tug forced her to hold on to past sorrows, hurts, losses and a disconnection from self-awareness.

She regretted that she'd just disclosed to a perfect stranger how lost she was in her life. But maybe that was the point. If you can confess your truths to someone you don't even know, perhaps you can begin to confront them for yourself, figure it all out, and grow. Or not. She felt confused and out of touch with rationality.

Information poured into her brain throughout the day. Uriel was good, comprehensive, an impressive communicator about both science and spirituality. He put everything into an understandable context that made sense. As a former microbiologist, a neuroscientist also trained in integrative medicine, Uriel put facts in digestible bite-sized nuggets for mass consumption. He discussed the biology of the human body, the neurosciences of the brain, and the science of the heart-brain connection. Robin was fascinated to learn that signals from the heart have a direct effect on brain function and influence emotions as well as cognitive abilities such as attention, perception and memory. By cultivating positive emotions, she could increase heart rhythm coherence, benefitting health and improving performance.

Using an illustrated, gigantic PowerPoint on the screen behind him, Uriel shared the impact of the stress response in both good and destructive ways. He talked about how the fight-or-flight mechanism is built into the amygdala in the brain and controls the release of hormones such as adrenaline and cortisol, which pump up the heart rate and propel energies into the limbs to deliver the strength to run or fight the predator.

"This magnificent system," extolled Uriel, "is meant for our survival so that we can live to fight another day." He explained that after we're safe, we're supposed to recover quickly from the rapid, amped-up breathing and racing heart. But many people live with high stress levels, which ultimately suppress non-essential functions such as digestion and the immune system. "Let's face it, if you're running from a hungry tiger, you're not worrying about digesting your last meal. You just don't want to become the ferocious beast's next meal, right?"

The crowd murmured and nodded heads in agreement.

"So, if you remain in stress for extended periods, chances are good you'll become ill. Your body stops functioning optimally. The fact is that 95% of visits to primary care physicians are for stress-related symptoms."

He talked about solutions, emphasizing the importance of aligning mind and body for homeostatic balance and well-being "to awaken your inner powers," he highlighted. He had acquired his wisdom from teachers he had worked with in India and Tibet. He had studied yoga and meditation, Tibetan medicine and Ayurveda. He was intent on sharing his knowledge to help his students release their struggles and embrace their unlimited potential.

Robin felt she had learned a great deal about mind-body alignment from her yoga training but was hopeful that Uriel would provide tangible motivation and an approach she could sustain.

He continued. "Life is play. Suffering is optional. We've become too serious, too self-defeating, too fearful. Fear and anxiety stop the flow of the vital life force, blocking energy and its infinite source. You can change," he asserted, pausing for effect. "You can learn to access your innate capabilities and transition gracefully from surviving to thriving. You are far more expansive than you realize."

The entire afternoon was bursting with mind-blowing, interactive strategies. He demonstrated specific ways to activate self-empowerment, to integrate mind and body in profound ways. He didn't just lecture about mindfulness, awareness, and consciousness, he guided students into interactive experiences. The exercises were miraculous, and he was hitting his stride, in the zone, like an NFL quarterback throwing one targeted touchdown after another. He was imposing and inspiring. Robin was riveted, hanging on every word, and engrossed by each evidence-based experience.

Uriel concluded with a preview of the next day's agenda. He planned to address the global influences of cycles affecting the planet and our lives. And he intended to share more techniques relating to lifestyle choices, illuminating how to live in harmony with life's polarities, the important pillars of health and balance, and the biological imperatives of food, movement, sleep, purpose, and love. Robin had a foundational understanding of the basic pillars of wellness by living in a Blue Zones community, but she was awed by the experiential lessons that were descending deeper into her consciousness. The day had already been packed with revelations. She was amazed at how much more Uriel planned to deliver.

Before finishing, Uriel was quick to point out that the techniques are only beneficial if they're used. "Practice is the secret to changing your life. If you find only one strategy over this entire weekend that resonates and works for you, stick with it vigilantly. Practice!" And with that, he opened both hands as if he were Atlas gathering the entire world in his arms and told the room, "Make it a great evening." He brought his palms together in front of his heart and reverently bowed in slow motion to the audience.

Robin felt a quiver of excitement roll through her body as she thought about dining with Yuri shortly. As others in attendance milled around in a stimulated state of chattiness, she took no time for niceties as she hurried back to her room to put on something casually chic and a little sexier. Her mind was submerged in spinning thoughts and emotions inspired by the intense training. But she was more unsettled by the anticipation of being with the master across a dining table. She pinched herself trying to separate the massive, superhuman screen image of Uriel Emanuel from the kind, attentive, man-sized Yuri of yesterday.

She took an invigorating shower and decided on a floral sundress with a low rounded neckline and strappy sandals with heels that gave her a taller appearance. She pulled the hairdryer from the wall to style a few curls into her chestnut locks that tumbled around her shoulders. Not being adept at makeup, she traced a thin outline of sapphire eyeliner to accent her copper-colored eyes and added a hint of blush to accent her high cheekbones. Satisfied, as if ready for her high school prom, she stepped back from the mirror. She was perspiring slightly even though she'd just showered, and the room was well air-conditioned. She was nervous and tense. She decided to use one of the relaxing breathing techniques she'd learned that afternoon.

Taking a slow, full breath in through her nose, she counted to six beats and then breathed out the same amount. She closed her eyes, concentrating on breathing in, breathing out. Focus on the rhythm. It's a circle. Breathing out all worries and fears. Breathing in calmness and divine love. What Uriel had said made perfect sense. "You cannot breathe in the past. You cannot take a breath in the future. Breathing connects you with now. You can only breathe in the moment." She liked that. She wanted to be in the moment...in the moment with him.

In the middle of her "practice," her phone buzzed, forcing her to open her eyes. A text from Yuri. Oh no, I hope he's not cancelling. Her mind automatically leaped into a negative thought, anticipating a rejection, and arousing disappointment. At the workshop, Uriel had talked about being mindful of thoughts since they profoundly affect the body. She stopped her disquieting, premature reaction to fully read the text.

"Beautiful Robin, when you come to the lobby, go to the concierge desk. A driver will meet you and take you to a special place where I'll be waiting. You said you like surprises! Yuri."

The message left Robin breathless. He addressed her as "beautiful." Is that what he thought? More obviously, he had taken time amid his busy teaching schedule to plan a surprise, something special just for her. She could barely contain her glee. A rush of excitement sent hot flashes into her head and she felt as if vibrations were pulsating through her entire body. Still staring at the message in total disbelief, she pressed Judy's number.

"Judy. I need someone to calm me down. Can we talk? Am I catching you at a good moment?"

Judy was eager to listen. Robin rapid-fired a complete update of the last 24 hours and the fact that she was now about to have a surprise dinner with this amazing mystical man at some undisclosed location.

When Robin paused finally to catch her breath, Judy broke into laughter.

"What's so funny?"

In a slow, tranquilizing voice, Judy told Robin that she deserved to have joy and what an exciting turn of events. She should just allow herself to appreciate the uniqueness of these experiences and take them all in without analyzing everything. "Go with the flow, my friend."

"Perfect!," Robin remarked, dripping with sarcasm.

CHAPTER SIXTEEN

*T*he young, tanned Uber driver with sleeves of tattoos on both arms was extremely talkative on the short ride and yet uncomfortably mum about where they were going.

"I'm letting him know we're five minutes away," Regis announced, picking up his phone. Robin assumed by him, he meant Yuri.

It was the golden hour when the sun lowered towards the horizon and produced warm, natural light with long, intriguing shadows. The diffuse radiance bathed the palm-treed landscape with a dreamlike softness. Finally, the Honda hatchback pulled into a marina. A marina! And there was Yuri walking briskly towards the car and opening the door like the true gentleman he was. He saluted Regis, waving him on and escorted Robin into his arms for a lingering hug. She could feel her cheeks blushing as she noticed herself leaning into his powerful presence. He had exchanged his button-down shirt for a casual black tee and Robin could feel its silky suppleness and his muscular chest.

"I'm very glad you like surprises," said Yuri, releasing her body and taking her hand to guide her onto a wooden dock. Her sandals had not been the most appropriate choice but who knew! She walked on her toes to avoid snagging her heels in the planked crevices.

"You're full of tricks, aren't you?" She gazed up at his radiant and soothing smile. He squeezed her hand.

"It's a beautiful evening for an adventure." He paused in front of a pretty, huge white sailboat and escorted Robin carefully on board where a rustic-looking guy with a white beard greeted them. "Meet my friend Captain Doug, owner of this magnificent trimaran."

"Awesome," uttered Robin, trying to take in the blur of everything at once. "Nice to meet you."

"Our captain is taking us for a little sunset cruise and his wife Amelia will whip up the tastiest and healthiest dinner you'll ever have at sea. An incomparable chef." He winked at Doug who suggested they make themselves comfortable on the aft deck, a veritable floating entertainment area. A long couch ran along the stern from starboard to port. The gracious dining table held two flutes containing a deep yellow-orange liquid. Yuri handed one to Robin. "A combination of mango, pineapple juice and a spritz of seltzer."

"This is so elegant," gushed Robin, toasting Yuri's glass of non-alcoholic beverage. They cozied into a blue fleece throw in the center of the couch, softening its hard vinyl surface.

"I love being outdoors. To be honest, I wanted privacy from students who would likely be at the area restaurants. This seemed a far better option," Yuri said.

"I'm not complaining," Robin joked, realizing that Captain Doug was at work unmooring the vessel and they had yet to set eyes on Amelia. They were alone on the deck, under azure skies with dots of stars beginning to emerge. Streaks of yellows and oranges whispered across the cirrus clouds with reflections bobbing on the rippling waters below.

"Did you enjoy today?," Yuri asked neutrally.

"Yes. Immensely. Synchronicity strikes again. I had no idea…"

"I'm pleased you're in the program. But let's leave that on shore for now. I want to hear more about your writing."

Robin dove into talking about her research on music, sound and the healing benefits of Solfeggio tones. Yuri seemed quite knowledgeable on the subject. "It's all about vibrations," he offered. "Energy."

Amelia climbed the short flight of stairs from the lower deck holding an enormous tray of delicious-looking appetizers. She was a big-boned woman with striking emerald eyes that looked out from a bronzed face, weathered from many sun-aging hours at sea. Long, kinky graying black hair was wrapped up into a heap on the back of her head. She looked older than her fifty years but had a kind, approachable confidence, totally at ease with who she was. Yuri made the introductions as he watched Amelia carefully place the delectable edibles within their reach. She explained that everything was made from scratch and she pointed out each treat. Butternut squash hummus on grain-free crackers. Guacamole with kale chips. A vegan seven-layer dip on dried apple slices. She also carried a pitcher of the mango-pineapple beverage and stood it in the middle of the table.

When she left, Yuri and Robin set about tasting the assorted items. One was more scrumptious than the next. "My tastebuds are exploding," Robin exclaimed approvingly of the creations.

Yuri explained that Amelia did private catering and when she wasn't booked, she and Captain Doug took couples for weekend sailing retreats.

"The sun is setting," announced Yuri as the boat was now skimming along undulating waves. The round, sinking ball of glowing oranges and reds was reflected on the surface of the ocean.

"Breathtaking," Robin admired.

Suddenly she turned to look Yuri squarely in the eyes.

"Yes?" He smiled, egging her on encouragingly.

"Can I ask a personal question?"

"Have at it," he responded openly.

"Why aren't you married?' She didn't intend to ask in such an accusatory way like something was wrong with him. Feeling embarrassed at blurting out such a blunt question, Robin began to blabber. "I mean you're so evolved, wise, kind, accomplished, handsome…" She paused, feeling herself digging a deeper hole of humiliation.

Yuri laughed, a warm reassuring chuckle that diminished the tension that had started to constrict her neck. She relaxed.

"I was married."

Robin waited patiently for more. Yuri took a gulp of his drink.

Impatient and unable to control herself, Robin asked, "Do you have children?"

"We were not blessed with children. We were going through an adoption when…" He paused again to breath evenly before continuing.

"My wife was killed in an accident. Head on by a drunk driver."

"Oh my, Yuri. I'm so sorry. I didn't mean…"

"No. It's okay. That was five years ago. I still grieve. I will always miss her. But it is the journey, both hers and mine. It is what it is. And you?"

Robin admitted that her marriage was not the best experience. "My husband was an unhappy man and I failed to make him happy. Then I realized that was beyond my job description," she laughed, noticing Yuri's irresistible grin in acceptance of her story.

At that moment, one of those "ah-ha" realizations slapped across her mind, something learned from the day's lectures. She was holding on to her stories and they influenced how she saw herself, her beliefs, perceptions and expectations. In her marriage, she saw failure, as if she were less than, lacking, an impostor. She had given undue value to these life accounts. In truth, they were merely an accumulation of experiences that could be better used to learn, grow and connect to deeper understandings about simply being human. She'd become too invested in examining, interpreting, and being hurt. She didn't like feeling vulnerable and steeled herself against the possibility of hurt and rejection. She had locked herself into a prison where she was missing life, viewing it from the sidelines as it rolled by. *I've been traumatized by my mother's disappearance.*

Yuri noticed her pensiveness. "Care to share?"

She giggled like a teenager and watched the bold colors on the horizon, nature's impressive light show.

She took a deep breath. "Nah. It's just an old story."

"I like old stories. They can lead to breakthroughs."

"Now don't go turning into Uriel Emanuel when I was just getting used to you being Yuri."

He chided her. "Yuri, at your service. Share with me."

Just then Amelia returned with Captain Doug. "Sorry to interrupt," she apologized. They carried glorious trays of copious foods, plates and more drinks.

"Are you joining us?" Yuri was overwhelmed by the quantity of entrees extravagantly laid out on the dining table.

"No. No." Captain Doug protested, putting up a defensive hand. "For you two to enjoy."

"Wow. Thank you," Robin effused.

Once again, Amelia spent a moment identifying the dishes: broccolini chickpea pizza, cauliflower steaks, a side of carrot crisps, spinach salad, and sweet potato pomegranate. Captain Doug put an arm around his wife's shoulder and they disappeared back through the cabin hole and down the stairs.

"Your story?" Yuri stared at Robin.

"Well..." she hesitated. "I understand loss." She went on to give him a Cliff Notes version of her mother's disappearance and her sister's trials and tribulations. In the middle of her sharing, Yuri commented about having a desire to visit Provence. "I'll have to add Arles to my bucket list," he said, gazing out to the vast ocean. Robin made a mental note to revisit that topic with Yuri.

Somehow Yuri had become the catalyst for Robin to expose the depths of all that she had dammed up inside for so long. He had strong broad shoulders, but it wasn't as if he were taking on her issues. He was merely helping her release them. He made no judgment, allowing her to blossom with the guidance of her own insights. Somewhere in the back of her mind, she remembered the predictions that old Hannah, the intuitive, had given. This moment resonated. This unusual man was bringing her to a different understanding of herself just by listening in his knowing way and allowing her to articulate her fears and worries.

Beneath them was the real Robin, her truth, her authenticity, her connection to a dimension that contributed to a feeling of resilience, even power. "You are more powerful than you realize," Hannah had said. Today, Uriel had echoed that when he said, "You are far more expansive than you realize. Truths."

She was in a groove. "And now allow me to present yet another example of synchronicity…" She reached into her purse and pulled out the book that had been inscribed to her mother. With unbridled gusto, holding nothing back, she presented it to Yuri.

He gawked at the cover with immediate recognition. "Oh my. Now that's an old story," he chortled.

"Do you remember?" Robin was on the edge of the seat. "Do you remember my mother? Ruth Stevens?" She put down her fork, stopped eating or drinking and waited agog for Yuri's response.

"That was a long time ago. The first workshop I ever taught. Less than a dozen students."

After an exceedingly long pause, he stated, "Life is amusing, isn't it? You never quite know what's around the next corner."

"And?" Robin's impatience was getting the best of her.

Yuri opened to read the autograph he had written to Ruth. "Yes, I remember her. I was still a relative kid back then, my first program. She was older, full of energy, smart, filled with dreams. She wanted to own the world. She was married with two kids.

He paused with a grin. "Ha, that would've been you and your sister." He searched his memories. "I remember she felt overwhelmed, a little stuck, like a lot of young mothers. She wanted to learn how to navigate and make the best of things. She was a willing student and did well...." He stopped. "I'm sorry she wasn't there for you. But that was her journey, not yours." Yuri's words burned through Robin.

Surprising herself with an enormously forward request, she proclaimed, "I need a Yuri hug," extending both arms, ready to receive his warmth. It was wholly unusual for her to ask for what she wanted. Yuri gleefully obliged. And suddenly, she was keenly aware of being present, in the moment, and a wave of contented exuberance swept through her from head to toe. They held each other for a long time, absorbing the happy vibe into their neural pathways. The sky had darkened to a star-studded composition. The air was cooler. There had been a monumental shift between them, a bonding. An astonishing connection. It was both invigorating and unsettling. "Thank you," Robin said, at last. "You've given me an amazing gift."

Yuri put his arm around her shoulders, holding her against him. "We're all in this together."

Amelia popped up out of the dimly lit lower deck and brought a small offering of desserts. Little shot glasses filled with mousses and creamy fruits that were all naturally sweetened with Medjool dates or stevia. "They're all healthy," she announced and asked, "Coffee or tea?"

"I'm good. Thank you. Wow, they look amazing," Robin managed.

"This was exquisite Amelia. Thank you. You've outdone yourself, especially on such short notice. I'm good, too," said Yuri.

"A pleasure! We should be docked in about 15 minutes," offered Amelia. "Excellent," replied Yuri.

Wrapped again in Yuri's arms, Robin was silent, listening to the murmur of the breeze, the strumming of the motor and the gentle splashing of waves. She and Yuri were blissfully absorbing this exceptional instant. Just being. Two souls fleetingly floating together, hearts joined, feeling safe and protected momentarily in the seas of life.

After extending profuse gratitude to the captain and chef, Yuri and Robin disembarked and hopped into an Uber to return to the hotel.

As they rode in the back seat of the car, Yuri announced, "I have to fly to New York right after the workshop tomorrow." Robin felt her heart collapse under the weight of this new piece of information. Her head spun. Old habits die hard. It's the old me reacting. Let go of attachments. Be grateful to Yuri. Practice holding onto that thought. She finally found her neutral mental gear so she could listen to him without a stream of emotional upheavals.

He continued, "But I have no bookings next weekend. May I come visit Naples and see you?" He sounded like a little boy asking if he could have his favorite ice cream. Her heart slipped into high gear, beating rapidly. It was too tough a challenge to remain unemotional. Finally, she whispered, "I'd like that." He leaned toward her, lifted her chin, and kissed her on the lips. It was not a long, passionate kiss but an expressive seal-the-deal kind of affection, a subtle hint of things to come.

As he bid her goodnight in the hotel lobby, he gave her one more of his famous Yuri hugs. "Sleep well. See you tomorrow," and he kissed her forehead gently.

Robin floated off to her room, ripped off her clothes, and fell into bed. It had been a very full, extremely long glorious day. A major shift day, as she would call it months later. She had no more real answers than she'd had that morning, but she had discovered an inner peacefulness, a fullness that allowed her to be whole and complete within herself. She looked forward to seeing Uriel Emanuel on stage and would accept whatever would come next weekend with Yuri and thereafter.

She finally felt as if she were owning her own power and was curious to see what would unfold next.

Communication with her higher self had been ignited. She was ready to courageously move forward to live fully with awareness and to give of herself unconditionally to others. Through her choices and her writings, she would facilitate change, awaken spirit and empower others. While life wasn't perfect, it was becoming perfect for her. She was ready to release all struggles, let go of the past, and pursue her passions to write, share and grow. She dissolved into a deep, restorative sleep. She would welcome the new dawn with open eyes and conscious enthusiasm.

~

EPILOGUE

Two years later, Yuri had his hand entwined in Robin's as they flew across the ocean on a direct flight to France. Marcel had happily planned a party in Arles to celebrate the newlywed's life together. Michelle Ruth, now 18, was actively involved in the orchestration of this wonderful event. Even Nan, Stephanie and their husbands were flying over for the occasion.

Robin still had ups and downs and awful knee-jerk reactions to situations from past losses. Old destructive thoughts still bubbled up in her mind. Slowly, she was liberating herself from old stories. A work in progress. These days she was more resilient, confident, and handled matters differently.

Yuri and Robin had been through monumental changes together over the last 24 months as they endured a global pandemic that shut down many of Yuri's workshops, forcing him to switch to virtual presentations. There were political and racial upheavals that impacted every aspect of their lives. But the world had now righted itself. People had uncovered reliable solutions to conflicts and cataclysmic changes. Challenges still needed to be confronted but more of the world's populations were accepting a unity of purpose and a shared consciousness more in alignment with ancient teachings, like what Yuri had been sharing with his students for decades. Thankfully, shifts were happening for the benefit of all humanity.

For Robin, the ultimate was that she was fully awake in her life. She didn't need Yuri to complete her, but the reality was that to love someone freely and completely as she loved Yuri, and being able to accept his love in return, felt miraculous. Although the real miracle was a new young life they were nurturing together. They had adopted precious Gloria Ann, an adorable 2-year-old who was now being temporarily spoiled by Robin's sister Jean and her husband Nathan in Amityville while Robin and Yuri were on their overseas excursion. At last, she had a relationship with her sister, not what she expected but she had learned that expectations are frustrations waiting to happen. She and Jean had accepted one another as they are now, not as what they were or what Robin imagined they should've been. They had something.

Robin was grateful to still feel connected to her mother, an energy that can never be extinguished. She knew now how much more we are than our physical form. Her mother was alive in the light in her eyes, especially the way she looked at Yuri and Gloria Ann, and the way she enjoyed her sister and close friends like Judy and Suzanne. The words her mother had shared in the locket that paved the road to Yuri had transformed her life. *An open heart lets in light and love.*

Robin and Yuri split their time between New York City and Naples. Robin sold her motorcycle and she and her groom had taken up sailing together. They'd bought a small sailboat, adoring the freedom of being on the water. Yuri's two golden retrievers were always the first on board and the first to dive into the Gulf waters. Gloria Ann always wore her pink water wings with delight.

Life was unfolding moment by moment and Robin was beaming inside and out. She leaned against Yuri and counted her blessings. The plane touched down and she heard herself blurt out in French, *On arrive.*

~

The End

~

*D*ear Reader,

I'm grateful to so many people who have been part of the journey to bring this novel to the light of day, from supportive friends to my life partner, Patrick. Friends stepped up in amazing ways.

Talented and spiritual Marilu Garbi, a superb artist, immediately created a series of cover designs, offering her personal butterfly painting which became the obvious selection. She also took on the book layout which required tedious editing revisions that she handled with remarkable aplomb. I'm so indebted to her for delivering the easy-to-read design with such steadiness and calm enthusiasm.

Beth Preddy, with whom I've long worked in her public relations capacity and have come to appreciate as a topnotch wordsmith, willingly accepted the editing task. Her personal insights, valuable changes and keen attention to detail brought the story to a far sweeter flow.

Special acknowledgements to those who read my first draft and offered treasured and encouraging feedback included Hazel Kandall, Rita Losee, Nancy MacDonald, Linda Mlacek, and M.J. Wagner. Special thanks to Caroline Thonon, who read the early chapters as they were being written while we shared a cabin in the North Georgia mountains. You are the ones who put the wind in my sails and words cannot adequately describe my elation at your graciousness.

Most of all, I'm appreciative to you, the reader, for being on this journey with me and my heart-felt characters.

Writing a novel has long been on my bucket list, but it took the 2020 pandemic to stop me in my tracks long enough to embrace the task. In the interest of transparency, in July, I also broke my arm climbing boulders to get a closeup video of a snowy white egret. I was sidelined when I had to have surgery. Ugh! Clearly that put a hitch in the giddyup. These unfortunate external circumstances forced me into retreat. By day, I was alone, isolated, and became submerged in my own world, disappearing into provocative thoughts which cultivated fertile ground for *Awakening* to emerge.

One steamy summer morning with my cup of black coffee in hand, I sidled up to the standing desk in my art-filled office to check emails on my desktop. Suddenly the title for this book flashed across my consciousness. *Awakening*. Simple. What does that mean? And now what?

Honestly, I just started writing, totally clueless as to where the plot was going. The story flowed as if from an outside source, a spiritual guide, a guardian. I was physically typing on the keyboard, but it wasn't me writing the words and I knew it. Rather than resisting, I enabled the process and just let it happen. I continually thanked the muse and mastermind.

As an avid reader, I'm addicted to page-turning novels, the ones you can't put down, where the characters and events are so engrossing that you almost feel a responsibility for the outcome. You become both curious and protective and there's an intimacy that develops. Those kinds of books become a total immersion, an escape from reality when you're utterly unaware that there's a global pandemic, social unrest, political chaos, or have your arm in a brace and can't play tennis with friends. You enter a different dimension, oblivious to the real world.

For me, that's how it felt to write this book. Every morning, I'd wake up so excited to get to my computer. I'd re-read the previous day's pages, wondering who had written them. As it came time to move the story forward, I'd have absolutely no idea what would unfold. Occasionally insecurities arose, and I'd worry that the muse would leave. But my guide always pumped fresh ideas through my mind's eye. I finished the first draft in just ten weeks.

The characters are all fictional, yet their experiences and emotions bubbled up from the depths of my soul. For me, writing this novel was cathartic and reflective. Robin's path can lead all of us to find purpose, explore relationships, and to connect to real love, our essence.

While essentially confined to my home, the book project gave me the opportunity to virtually travel all over the world, to places I have personally visited in the past. Others I researched (thank you, Google!). Claustrophobic impulses, feeling trapped or out of touch, quickly dissipated and I dissolved into adventurous experiences. Plus, I was still doing my other work projects and also coaching clients, which brings me to another confession.

As a personal development coach trained in eastern and western traditions, my hidden agenda was to infuse some of my teachings into these pages. My hope has been to convey insights and motivation to spur you on to navigate your own path to a happier life.

I would be delighted to connect with you. Please take a moment to write a review on Amazon. It would mean a lot to me and I read every one! Subscribe to my newsletter. Join my Facebook page, visit my website. Join the Awakening Facebook group for inspiration on life's journey.

Or feel free to send me questions or comments at

Peggy@PeggySealfon.com

I will happily respond.

I'm humbled to be able to share this writing with you and sincerely wish for you to carve your own personal path to empowerment and contentment.

Love and Light,

Peggy Sealfon

AwakeningANovel.com
PeggySealfon.com

*P*eggy Sealfon is a lifelong wordsmith, entrepreneur, author, and personal development coach trained in eastern and western traditions. Raised in the oceanfront community of Neponsit, in Queens, New York, she spent her late teens and twenties in New York City's Greenwich Village, commuting around town on a motorcycle. A serial entrepreneur, she followed a path from being a journalist writing for such prestigious publications as the *New York Times* to owning retail shops in Princeton, New Jersey to running an advertising agency in Southwest Florida to life coaching clients around the world. Her best-selling non-fiction book is *Escape From Anxiety–Supercharge Your Life With Powerful Strategies From A to Z*. Always fascinated by human nature, Peggy believes in the infinite potential of resilience, adaptability and creativity. A seeker of truths, Peggy is passionate about guiding others towards higher levels of physical, mental and emotional well-being. She resides in Naples, Florida on the Gulf of Mexico with her life partner, Patrick.

CPSIA information can be obtained
at www.ICGtesting.com
Printed in the USA
BVHW041040110221
599916BV00009B/690